PARADISE

Passion in
Paradise

Awakening

JACI BURTON

ELLORA'S CAVE
ROMANTICA PUBLISHING

An Ellora's Cave Romantica Publication

www.ellorascave.com

Paradise Awakening

ISBN 1843606127, 9781843606123

This book printed in the U.S.A. by Jasmine-Jade Enterprises, LLC.

Trade paperback Publication June 2003

Content Advisory:

S – ENSUOUS
E – ROTIC
X – TREME

Ellora's Cave Publishing offers three levels of Romantica™ reading entertainment: S (S-ensuous), E (E-rotic), and X (X-treme).

The following material contains graphic sexual content meant for mature readers. This story has been rated E–rotic.

S-*ensuous* love scenes are explicit and leave nothing to the imagination.

E-*rotic* love scenes are explicit, leave nothing to the imagination, and are high in volume per the overall word count. E-rated titles might contain material that some readers find objectionable — in other words, almost anything goes, sexually. E-rated titles are the most graphic titles we carry in terms of both sexual language and descriptiveness in these works of literature.

X-*treme* titles differ from E-rated titles only in plot premise and storyline execution. Stories designated with the letter X tend to contain difficult or controversial subject matter not for the faint of heart.

Also by Jaci Burton

ℵ

About the Author

&

In April 2003, Ellora's Cave foolishly offered me a contract for my first erotic romance and I haven't shut up since. My writing is an addiction for which there is no cure, a disease in which strange characters live in my mind, all clamoring for their own story. I try to let them out one by one, as mixing snarling werewolves with a bondage and discipline master can be very dangerous territory. Then again, unusual plotlines offer relief from the demons plaguing me.

In my world, well-endowed, naked cabana boys do the vacuuming and dishes, little faeries flit about dusting the furniture and doing laundry, Wolfgang Puck fixes my dinner and I spend every night engaged in wild sexual abandon with a hunky alpha. Okay, the hunky alpha part is my real-life husband and he keeps my fantasy life enriched with extensive "research". But Wolfgang won't answer my calls, the faeries are on strike and my readers keep running off with the cabana boys.

Jaci welcomes comments from readers. You can find her website and email address on her author bio page at www.ellorascave.com.

Tell Us What You Think

We appreciate hearing reader opinions about our books. You can email us at Comments@EllorasCave.com.

PASSION IN PARADISE:
PARADISE AWAKENING

෨

Acknowledgement

ॐ

This is my first book and I have many people to thank for getting me here, so bear with me through this lengthy acknowledgement.

A big thank you to my critique partners, Mel, Jodi and Jamie, who make anything I write look good. Without you, I wouldn't have gotten this far.

To the FY gang, thank you for letting me whine and complain and thanks for always making me laugh. You're my refuge.

To my editor, Briana St. James — you've been a godsend to me and I'm so lucky to have you for an editor. Thank you for your positive encouragement and guidance through this process.

To my mother, who always believed in me and told me I could do anything I set my mind to do — thanks, Mom!

For my kids — Kevin, Matt and Ashley, for your support and for loving me no matter what.

And most importantly, to Charlie, my husband and my love. Without your love, patience and encouragement I'd never have done this. Thank you for helping me reach for the stars. This book is dedicated to you, babe. You're my everything.

Chapter One

ജ

Michael Donovan finished unpacking and headed straight to the wet bar in the suite's living room. He poured whiskey into the tumbler and downed it in one swallow.

Ahh, the sweet burn. Maybe he'd just drink himself into oblivion tonight.

He knew better than to have relationships with women. He just wasn't any damn good at them. Ginny was just the latest example of his failure to even remotely understand the feminine mind. He'd be much better off to steer clear of anyone bearing estrogen for the week he was at this resort.

He'd started to pour another glass of whiskey when the doorknob rattled and a sound like someone fiddling with the lock caught his attention.

Great. Housekeeping. They could bring more whiskey. He threw open the door, ready to tell the maid to keep the liquor cabinet stocked.

The woman standing there was no maid. He didn't know if she was part of the amenities of Paradise Resort or not, but she sure beat the hell out of a gift basket. No gift basket had ever made his cock twitch.

Her generous mouth hung open in surprise. He waited for her to speak.

Nothing. Not that it was a problem. He'd be perfectly happy to while away a few minutes staring at the curly blond hair piled on top of her head, those cute wire rimmed glasses that couldn't hide her sea green eyes, and watch her lick her lips with a tongue that already had his mind whirling in thoughts of sex and sweat.

Sex. Too bad Ginny had backed out at the last minute. Fucking fashion models! So skinny her hip bones stabbed him when they fucked. So he'd just spend time doing research on his next book. Too bad he wouldn't have the live, female version of research to help him on his way. Not a girlfriend, not a woman he actually had to pay attention to. Just a fucking partner. No strings attached.

Like the one standing in front of him. Beautiful face and expressive eyes, but she wasn't really his type. Too bookish and her clothes fit too loose. And she was possibly mute.

"Can I help you?" he finally asked.

"I . . . uh, I. . ." She shuffled back and forth, her arms laden with what looked like a huge backpack. Dressed in linen pants and a loose blouse, she surely couldn't be hotel staff. He tilted his head sideways, trying to imagine what kind of body she hid under those clothes.

"Are you lost?" he asked.

"I don't think so. This is room ten, right?"

Michael scanned the door. "That's what it says."

"Then, um, I think there's been some mix-up."

"Why?"

"Because this is my room."

He laughed. "No, this is *my* room."

"I have a key," she said, holding out the white plastic thing that hotels nowadays insisted on using. He missed regular keys.

"I can see that. But this is still my room."

She blew a stray curl off her face. "Could I put this stuff down for a minute? These bags are heavy."

"Sure." He grabbed for the bag and almost dropped it to the ground. "Jesus, what do you have in this thing? Rocks?"

"No," she said, rolling her shoulders now that the weight had been lifted from them. "They're my books."

Paradise Resort offered every erotic amenity, and the woman brought books? Interesting. Then again, he'd brought his laptop, but that was because this was more or less a research trip for his next book – he wasn't here to indulge in the sexual amenities the resort provided.

Correction – he had planned to indulge in sex with Ginny, before she conveniently remembered that she had a shoot booked in Bali this week. More likely she was bored having him as her boy-toy-du-jour and had already found another stud to satisfy her. Fine with him. He was getting a bit bored with her anyway.

"Come on in," he said, "and we'll get this figured out."

She peered in, before gingerly stepping a few inches inside the door. He stifled a laugh at her timidity. She sure didn't fit the mold of what he was led to believe were the usual type of guests here. Bold, adventurous, forward – those were the types of people he expected to see this week. This one looked like a librarian. A librarian with a sexy mouth.

"Thanks. I don't know what's happened, but I'm sure the resort can figure it out." She was nervous, her eyes darting every which way.

"Relax. I'll call downstairs and have the manager find you another room. Take a look around if you want."

She nodded and headed toward the balcony overlooking the water. The ocean breeze whipped at her hair, blond tresses flying every which way.

Holy shit! She had some body hidden under those clothes. He almost dropped the phone when the wind pressed her blouse against generous, full breasts. Straining nipples appeared ready to poke through the silky blouse. Hips made for a man's hands swelled against her pants.

Fuck. It had been too damn long since he'd been with a woman. Damn Ginny and her globe trotting trips. Ah, hell, it was over between them anyway. The sex had been fun, but the girl was the biggest airhead. And once he got out of bed, it

11

would be nice to have an intelligent conversation with a woman.

He'd yet to find one who could satisfy both his sexual and intellectual appetites. That hadn't happened since he'd been with Mari. He thought he'd found everything with her. What he'd ended up with was a one way ticket to misery and divorce. Never again. Women were for fucking and fun. Not forever.

The woman on his balcony had double Ds written all over her. And not just her breasts – she was *desirable*, which made her *dangerous* to him.

He quickly dialed the manager, hoping to get "Double D" out of his suite as quickly as possible.

Serena Graham stared at the man on the phone, her heart racing. She'd almost dropped her bundles when he'd opened the door. First, he'd scared her to death because she hadn't expected anyone to be in her room. And second, he was an Adonis. Dark hair fell in unruly waves against the back of his neck like that movie star she drooled over all the time. He even had the same intense blue eyes, the kind that pierce right through you as if they can see inside your thoughts. Hopefully this man didn't have a mind connection to her – she'd die if he knew how she admired him.

Too bad she wasn't gutsy enough to ask him to help her.

"Bad news," he said after he hung up the phone.

She turned and watched him walk towards her. "Bad news?"

"They double booked this room. And the hotel is full for the week."

This could not be happening to her. She'd scrimped and saved part of her salary for over a year, bound and determined to grab some sexual excitement for once in her life. She'd read up on all the hedonistic resorts, and Paradise was the best. Unfortunately, it was also the only resort on this small island. She wasn't even sure she could get a flight back to the mainland today. What was she supposed to do? Sleep at the little airstrip until the next plane arrived?

"I see." Despair filled her. She sank into one of the cushioned chairs and buried her head in her hands. "Give me a minute and I'll get out of your way."

He studied her and seemed to be considering something. Probably how quickly he could get her out of his room.

She wasn't a sex siren. She wasn't the type of girl men fell over themselves to get close to. This whole trip was going to be a disaster. What had she been thinking? That she'd suddenly transform the minute she stepped onto the island?

Professor Serena Graham from a small Midwestern college was way out of her league with movie-star-man. Changing her clothes and putting on a front of sexual experience wasn't going to fly. Her inexperience would quickly trip her up.

What a mess. Maybe she should just give up and grab the next plane home.

"You don't have to leave, you know."

She raised her head, not sure she'd heard him right. "Excuse me?"

"I have an idea."

"An idea?"

"Are you meeting someone here at the resort?"

"Me?" Her eyes widened. "No. I came alone."

"Then you can stay here with me."

He was joking, right? She looked at him, all of him, from his wide shoulders and slim waist to the muscular thighs straining against his shorts. He was way more man than she knew how to handle.

But wait. Isn't that what she wanted? Someone to touch her in a way she'd never been touched before? Someone to throw her down and fuck her the way she'd been dying to be fucked? She wanted adventure, fantasy and hot, unbridled sex. Why not with this guy?

No, stupid idea. Very stupid. "Oh, I couldn't."

"Why not? This suite has two bedrooms. I won't get in your way if you don't get in mine. Think of us as roommates."

Roommates. A thought sailed through her mind, but she quickly brushed it away. Having anonymous sex was one thing. Having it with someone she'd be sharing a room with for a week was another matter entirely. Then again, at least she'd have a place to stay. And most of the "activities" occurred in the specialized rooms, not in the resort's bedrooms. At least that's what the brochure had said.

"If you're sure you don't mind?"

His gaze seemed to penetrate her clothes, making her feel like she was sitting there naked instead of completely covered.

"I don't mind at all."

Deep and husky, his voice stabbed at her middle, heat and liquid desire pooling together and making her squirm. Maybe this wasn't such a good idea.

Then again, maybe it was. "Thanks. I'll do it."

"Michael," he said holding out his hand.

She stood. "Serena." His warm hand sent little electric shocks through her. Funny, that had never happened before when she'd shaken any guy's hand. Her body trembled, her pussy tingled and flared to life as if to scream out, "This one! Choose this one!" He was dangerous and sexy and made her feel dangerous and sexy, too.

He'd be the kind of man who'd take whatever he wanted from a woman. Fire her up and make her burn for him. Make her scream his name when she reached the pinnacle, then beg him for more.

C'mon Serena. This isn't a movie. The good looking guy isn't going to pick you out of a crowd and make your dreams come true. And he sure as hell isn't going to make you come until you scream.

The only way she was going to get some hot and heavy action was to do it herself, just like always. It wasn't like she was inexperienced in these matters. She just didn't get the right guys. She got the losers. The ones who couldn't find their way to her pussy without a road map, and once there hadn't a clue what to do with it.

Okay, time to think logically and intellectually about this. She'd wanted some hot, unbridled passion, and right now the hottest guy she'd ever met had just become her roommate for the week.

"Are you here alone?" she asked.

He nodded, then frowned. "Why?

"Why would you come here by yourself?" She had thought her being alone would make her a minority.

"I could ask you the same question," he said, folding well-muscled arms across his broad chest.

She licked her lips, her gaze riveted to the dark hairs peeking above the top of his shirt. Her nipples tightened and she silently thanked the fashion gods for loose tops. Although the wardrobe she'd brought with her would put her, so to speak, front and center, with nothing to hide. She hoped she could handle it. No, she *had* to handle it.

"I didn't want any entanglements this week," she lied, hoping she'd sound worldly and sophisticated. Definitely not how she felt. It was the clothes. Once she changed clothes, her personality would follow suit.

He nodded. "I understand. Want to play around a little, do ya?"

She had no idea what she really wanted. But she'd never tell him that. "Yes, that's it."

"Well, take the bedroom down the hall to the left. I'll call the hotel manager and let her know you'll be staying with me."

"I'll pay for half the cost, of course," she said, gathering up her backpack.

He stepped towards her and took the pack from her hands, following her down the hall. "Not necessary. I've got it covered. I'll have your luggage brought up here. Then you can unpack and make yourself at home."

She turned and placed her hand on his chest. It was like touching fire. He burned her instantly and she almost pulled away. Almost. But he felt good, dammit. She didn't want to pull away. She wanted more. "I want to pay for my share of the room. It's only fair." Then, noticing how his eyes lingered where her hand rested, she quickly pulled it away. Okay, so she wasn't as brave as she'd like to think she was.

"Up to you. I'll go make that call."

She nodded and closed the door behind him. The room was lovely, with tropical flowers embroidered on the bedspread. The white furnishings reminded her of a paradise bungalow. Then again, that's what this place touted itself as – paradise. Depending on the type of paradise one searched for, of course.

After her luggage arrived, she unpacked her things, feeling a giddy excitement at the games she'd play over the next week. Hot, sexy games. With a lot of different guys. No, maybe just one. She wasn't promiscuous, just horny. At tonight's introductory cocktail party she'd scout out the merchandise and choose one that got her juices flowing. Which right now could be any guy with a penis.

Would all the men be as hot looking as Michael? Probably not. And why was he here alone? Did he expect to find a woman to play with? Maybe she should make the offer before the party tonight. After all, he certainly fit her criteria. Tall, bronzed like a Greek god, incredibly good looking. And she was certain he could satisfy her, judging by the way her panties moistened just thinking about him.

She imagined the two of them together — what they'd do. What would Michael be like as a sex partner? Would he be willing to indulge her fantasies? Or would he expect her to lie still while he fucked her?

No. That's what she'd experienced before. Plain, no frills, vanilla sex. Nothing in it for her but a few moments of anticipatory excitement before the man came and she didn't. That's what she found in Kansas. Not at Paradise Resort. Satisfaction guaranteed, they'd told her. And she was planning on ending the week-long stay extremely satisfied.

Maybe she would start with Michael. Why not? If she was going to transform herself into a brave, wanton sex siren, what better place to start than with a man who'd already gotten her hot without even touching her?

* * * * *

Michael felt better after a shower. It had been a long damn day, and he hadn't gotten a lick of work in yet. Not that his editor would hound him. He always made his deadlines. Besides, all he had left was finishing up edits for his latest erotic crime novel, and he'd shoot that to the editor within a week. She'd be happy as a woman at a shoe store. He'd have plenty of time to research his new book, which was why he was at Paradise Resort in the first place.

Oh sure, he thought he might get some serious fuck time in with Ginny while here, but that wasn't going to happen. And he sure as hell wasn't going to pick up one of the desperate-for-sex bunnies that populated places like this. He didn't have time for entanglements with women he didn't know. God help him should one glom onto him during this stay. Shooting mental warnings for his cock to behave itself, he picked up the resort brochure and scanned the events listing, shaking his head.

Sadomasochism Palace, Voyeurism Venture, every single one of the events screamed sex and multiple orgasms. The place didn't lie — they catered to all kinds of sexual enjoyments, from the plain to the perverse. No matter what you craved, Paradise Resort would satisfy.

"Find anything you like?"

Michael turned to the sound of Serena's voice. The pamphlet slipped from his hands and fluttered to the floor. Christ! She swayed into the room like a princess who knew every man's eyes were on her. Curvy hips, lush breasts, the whole package slammed him right between the legs. His balls tightened and he broke out into a sweat like an adolescent popping his first girlfriend's bra open. Was he drooling? He wiped his lip, unable to tear his eyes away from her.

Where had the dowdy woman in loose clothes gone? The one wearing glasses, whom he'd thought was somewhat plain?

She was gone. Kidnapped. Replaced by a goddess in a tight fitting, strapless, bright orange flowered…Kleenex!

"Uh, wow." Couldn't he manage even a third grade level vocabulary? He bit back a groan as she slinked toward him, the dress so tight it outlined every curve of the body she'd tried to hide earlier. Hidden no longer, her full breasts nearly spilled over the top of the dress. And legs! Jesus, the woman had legs. Long, tanned, slender — the kind of legs he loved. The kind with a little muscle and shape to them, the kind a man wanted wrapped around him while he drove into her wet, willing pussy.

Thankfully he had a shirt on. His cock, the one he'd told to behave earlier, wasn't listening. Rock hard and ready, it was desperately twitching in Serena's direction. No doubt trying to signal her for immediate mouth-to-cock assistance.

She smiled at him. "So, you're saying, or maybe not saying, that my new look is acceptable?"

Did she have to purr when she spoke? He kind of liked that stumbling stammering she'd done earlier. It was safe, at least. This, this just wasn't fucking fair.

"You look, uh, fine. Nice. Real nice."

She pursed her lips, drawing his attention to her mouth. Instinct told him to reach between his legs and massage the burgeoning ache. He fought desperately to ignore that urge. Damn, she tempted him with that mouth. Those full, painted lips. The kind a man wanted wrapped around his aching heat, sucking and pulling a screaming, gut-wrenching orgasm out of him.

"Thanks. You dropped this."

She crossed in front of him and bent down to retrieve the brochure. Christ, what an ass! Firm and round and perfectly shaped. Not flat, but nice and round and firm, just the way he liked it. Abso-fucking-lutely perfect. He laid his head in the palms of his hands, wishing he could take back the offer to share the suite with her. This week was going to be hell. A living, nightmarish, ball-crushing hell.

"Oh, the brochure!" she exclaimed, tracing the events listing with a long, manicured nail. She slipped onto the cushioned sofa, her bare thigh sliding against his naked leg. He resisted the urge to scoot away from her. "See anything in here you like?"

Where was his tongue? He couldn't form a word to save his life. "I'm, uh, not participating this week."

"What do you mean?" she asked, her pert, upturned nose crinkling with her frown.

"I'm here to research a book I'm working on. This isn't a pleasure trip for me."

"Oh." She cast her luscious lashes downward, and had the gall to look disappointed. "That's too bad."

"Why?"

She looked at him, those sea green eyes of hers pleading innocently. Innocent his ass.

"I was going to ask you a favor."

"What kind of favor?"

"About this week." She half turned, her breasts pushing up against the top of the dress. Damn, they were luscious. He bet his shaft would slide easily between the two full mounds, fucking them until he came all over that beautiful face.

Down cock, down. "What about this week?"

"Well, I came here for some action, Michael. And I was thinking, since we'll be sharing a room and all, that you and I could participate together in the, uh, events."

"Participate? How?"

She swallowed. "You know how. The way the brochure described."

"Well, I'm not really sure what you're getting at."

"C'mon, Michael," she said, her voice low and throaty and sexy as hell. "Don't make me spell it out for you."

So she was still a little shy. Definitely not what he expected at this resort. "If you want something from me, you're gonna have to spell it out, Serena. Tell me exactly what you want."

A brief glimpse of that unsure woman who'd all but stumbled into his room today surfaced, but she disguised it brilliantly with a quick lick of her hot, pink tongue over her lips.

"I'd like you to be my partner this week, Michael. I'd like us to choose events to participate in together. Events where we'd touch, kiss, explore each other's bodies. I want to suck you and feel your tongue on me. I want to feel that hot cock of yours deep inside me, pumping away until we both come."

Well, that sure as hell spelled it out for him.

Chapter Two

ဆာ

"I see." All too clearly, in fact, Michael's mind was awash in images of what he and Serena could do over the next week. No, no, no. Absolutely not. He was not about to get involved with a sex-starved woman this week, when what he really needed to do was research his book. If Ginny were here it would have been uncomplicated. Once the sex was over, she'd either sleep or lay in the sun. God forbid they should carry on a conversation. But Serena? No way.

He'd have to pay attention with her, not to mention engage in sexual activities that would rob his brain of even the rudimentary fundamentals of how to plot a book. Already the blood had rushed to his straining cock and he'd lost ten IQ points.

"Well? What do you think of my idea?" she asked.

He wasn't buying that innocent bat of her eyelashes for one second, despite the fact his penis jumped up and down and shouted, *Yes! Yes! Yes!* "I think it's a really bad idea. Like I said, I'm here to research, not participate."

Her expression softened and she cast her eyes downward, those long lashes fluttering against her cheek. "Oh."

Ah, hell. That damn hurt look from a woman always affected him. Serena was especially good at it. Her sad, puppydog face was like a knife in his heart. He wanted to pull her into his lap and stroke her back and tell her everything was going to be okay. And then fuck her senseless until she smiled again.

Not a bad plan, actually. "Hey, I didn't mean I wasn't attracted to you. I just have to concentrate on my work."

"It's okay," she said, quickly standing and walking toward the sliding glass doors open to the balcony. She turned to him. "What kind of books do you write?"

"Erotic crime novels."

She stared back at him for a second and tilted her head, then her eyes widened. "I read erotic crime novels. Only one Michael that I'm aware of. You wouldn't be Michael Donovan, would you? "

He nodded. "Yeah." For some reason the fact that she knew who he was surprised the hell out of him. She didn't seem the type to read his kind of books.

"I love your books," she said, a smile curving her lips before she turned back to view the ocean.

"Thanks. What do you do, Serena?"

"I'm a professor of literature at a small college in Kansas."

A professor? Hell, she didn't look old enough to be out of college yet, let alone be teaching at one. "No shit."

She didn't answer, seemingly miles away as she stared outside.

In profile, she was stunning. Hell, frontways, behind, sideways, she knocked his socks off. The face of an angel and the body of a seductress. A combo that would make any man's cock stand at attention. His certainly was. Making it through the week with a constant hard-on wasn't going to help his research one bit.

Then again, the protagonist of his newest book would be suffering severe sexual teasing from the femme fatale out to get him. Maybe it would be good research to be strung up tighter than a thinly stretched wire.

"I guess I should head downstairs and make some connections before all the single guys are taken for the week," she sighed.

Suddenly, the thought of her making connections with any guy's cock other than his irritated him. Big time.

But why? She wasn't his. Hell, he barely knew her. But what he'd seen showed an intelligent, beautiful woman that maybe, just maybe, might fit the main femme fatale in his new book. He could always chalk it up to research.

Yeah, right. Any excuse to find out exactly what she wasn't wearing under that tight little dress.

"Wait a second." He stood and walked over to her.

She turned to him and offered a delicate smile. God, she was breathtaking. Just like the woman he envisioned as the murderer in his new book. Beautiful on the outside, vicious killer on the inside. His mind churned with plot ideas, thinking he'd just found the perfect model for his heroine.

"Is it too late to change my mind about your offer?"

She lifted a brow. "You mean…?"

He nodded. "The more I think about it, the more I'm convinced you might be the perfect woman to help me with research for my next book."

She smiled, showing white, even teeth. "Oh, you mean it? I'd love that. I mean, I love your books; the characters are so psychotically perfect. I've studied your craft for years, Michael. I'd love to help."

He laughed, and couldn't help the tiny jolt of pride he felt that she thought so highly of his writing. "Thanks. But I didn't mean just the research for the book."

"I know that. You want to fuck me."

There went his cock again, like a divining rod and she held the water source. "Yes. I want to fuck you. I want to do a lot of things with you. Are you game?"

She nodded. "Yes. And thank you, Michael. You won't be disappointed."

"I'm sure I won't," he replied, lifting a blonde curl. She gasped when his knuckles brushed the top of one burgeoning breast. Her skin was like soft butter. His cock was demanding attention. *Patience, dammit.* It'll happen soon enough. Right now, he wanted to anticipate the moment when he revealed the secrets Serena barely hid underneath that scrap of dress.

"I have one condition, though," he said.

"What's that?"

"This week between us is about sex. Physical pleasure only. No emotions. No involvement. And nothing goes beyond this week. When the party's over, it's over forever."

She tilted her head to the side and her hair fell behind her back, giving him a clear view of that creamy neck. Damn he'd like to leave a few marks on that gorgeous throat of hers.

"Got it. Physical only. Sex only. No emotions. Exactly what I was thinking. You've got a deal, Michael." Her body practically thrummed with the excitement that showed so clearly on her face. He could feel the vibrations already. So could his penis. He might have to get a hammer and beat the bastard into submission.

Which conjured up all kinds of visuals on how Serena could tame his wayward penis.

He nodded. "Let's go downstairs and have a drink and see what fun they have in store for us this week."

Michael followed her out, watching her perfect ass sway back and forth as she headed towards the lobby. Hopefully, he wouldn't be the only man in attendance tonight with a hard-on like a steel beam.

* * * * *

Serena couldn't believe her good luck. She'd stumbled onto the perfect man for her foray into sexual paradise, and he'd just agreed to act as her stud for the week.

No, that sounded crass. But true. It wasn't like this was the Dating Game. It was sex. Rowdy, public or private, in groups or one-on-one, any way you wanted it sex. And she had to get it straight in her mind. She couldn't expect anything to come of this week except pure sexual enjoyment. Otherwise she'd be grossly disappointed.

Michael Donovan. Wow. She'd loved every single one of his books, read them with guilty pleasure in the privacy of her little apartment. She could only imagine what the university faculty would think if they knew she read erotic novels, especially ones like Michael wrote. Not only loaded with graphic sex, but psychopaths, serial killers, evil most profound. She inhaled his novels like she would forbidden fruit.

And did his writing ever turn her on. She'd masturbated to a few of his sex scenes before, vividly imagining the cop or agent who'd fallen under the spell of the beautiful, tormented, female with a body to die for and the psyche of a killer. Those scenes never failed to take her to new heights of sexual pleasure. Many times she had to muffle her screams as she came, knowing the walls of her apartment were too thin to be yelling out in ecstasy.

He had a wickedly sexual mind. Serena wondered if his mind traveled in those directions in his real life, or were those scenes he wrote about merely an exercise in literary creativity.

She'd bet he knew exactly what to do with a woman. Even more so than before, her excitement level grew in anticipation of the wild week ahead of her. Gone was mousy and plain Professor Graham. In her place, Sexy Siren Serena had materialized.

At least for the next week.

Michael led the way toward the throng of people already assembled in the resort lobby. Tropical flowers in tall urns decorated every corner of the dimly lit room. A huge bar sat against one wall, and the open deck on the ocean side blew a fragrant evening breeze inside the nearly packed room. Rattan tables and chairs circled the room, with plenty of space left over for standing and mingling.

The party was in full swing. People with drinks in hand were laughing and talking loudly. Hopeful and disappointed expressions could be seen in every group. There was even some graphic touching of women's asses and palming of men's crotches. Serena inhaled, mentally preparing herself for an adventure the likes of which she'd only dreamed.

Michael headed to the bar to get them drinks. Serena found an unoccupied table and grabbed two chairs. She hadn't been alone for more than a minute when a good looking man approached her. In his early thirties, she'd estimate—roughly the same age as Michael. He had sandy blonde hair, brown eyes and quite a nice physique. Muscular and well built. She'd guess he was involved in athletics or sports of some kind.

"Hi," he said, sliding into the seat she'd held for Michael. "My name is Steve."

She shook the hand he offered. "Hi, Steve. I'm Serena."

"This your first time here?"

"As a matter of fact it is. Why? Do I have that first-timer look about me?"

He laughed. "Nah. I come here a lot, so I know most of the regulars already."

"Oh, I see." He seemed like a decent enough guy. And if she hadn't already finagled a week with Michael as her partner, she might have considered Steve. But as it was, she had a feeling she'd have her hands full with the man she selected.

Then again, the brochure said that swapping and multiple partners was welcomed and encouraged at the resort. Maybe for others, but she'd be happy to share some mind blowing sex with just one guy.

"So, have you partnered off with anyone yet?" he asked.

Serena nodded. "Yes, I have. As a matter of fact, here he comes now."

Steve followed Serena's gaze to Michael. She smiled, watching Michael frown as he approached the table and set down the drinks. Jealous, maybe? No, that couldn't be it. Jealousy would imply emotional attachment to her, and he'd already made his "no emotion" speech.

"Michael, this is Steve." She made the introductions, noticing the two men sizing each other up as they warily shook hands. This could be fun. She'd never had two guys vying for her before.

Michael shot her a look that she couldn't quite decipher. She couldn't tell if he was pissed off or merely curious at Steve's presence.

"So, you two have partnered off for the week?" Steve asked, vacating the chair.

Michael spoke first. "Yeah, we have."

"Interested in a three-way?"

Oh my. Serena hadn't thought of that before. Did she even want two men at once?

"No thanks," Michael countered before she could say a word.

Guess not, then.

"No harm, no foul," Steve said. "I'll go scout out some other action. You two have fun this week."

After he walked away, Michael sat and pulled his chair as close to Serena's as physically possible. He *was* jealous. Or something. Either way, she liked it.

"Did you want a three-way with him?" he asked, his dark blue eyes focused intently on her.

Did she want one? She shrugged. "I have no idea. I've never had one."

"Trust me. They're not all that great."

Interesting. She made a mental note to explore that conversation some other time.

"Attention everyone. Can I have your attention please?"

They turned to the makeshift dais where a gorgeous woman stood. Dressed in a flowing, tropical sarong, she was a true goddess. Her shoulder-length red hair seemed alive in the evening light, the spotlights' glow showcasing her vivid blue eyes. Her body would make any man salivate. Full, high breasts, a tiny waist and slender hips. One long, tanned leg peeked out from a high slit in the side of her sarong.

"I'm Morgan Brown, the manager of Paradise Resort. Welcome to a week of passion, excitement, and any sexual adventure you could possibly desire."

Serena shifted, feeling the rush of excitement as the week she'd scrimped and saved for was about to begin.

Morgan continued. "I'll start with laying out a few ground rules. Really, there aren't many, except to indulge your fantasies to your heart's content. The only cardinal rule the resort holds is that if you are uncomfortable in any situation, the game stops. No one will force you to do anything you do not want to do."

She paused for emphasis. "Anyone who pressures another guest or harms them in any way will be forever banned from the resort, and turned over to the local authorities. We take our guests' safety very seriously here, and as long as the fun is mutual, you may enjoy yourselves with no limit."

"Please take a moment to scan the brochure and form on the tables. Select your adventures for the week, and turn them in at the desk before you leave tonight. Tomorrow, the fun begins. Enjoy your stay at Paradise Resort, and if you need anything at all, don't hesitate to ask me or one of the staff. "

Serena picked up the brochure, which described in great detail the different scenarios the resort offered. She supposed she'd need Michael's input, too, since he would have to share them with her.

What were his sexual tastes? Did he prefer plain sex, or something out of the ordinary? Hopefully he wouldn't want to do anything she found unpleasant.

"Let's take a look and make our choices," he suggested, his shoulder brushing against the side of her breast.

She inhaled, both anticipation and fear swirling inside her. She was about to embark on a sexual escapade with a complete stranger.

"Unless you're incredibly kinky and enjoy extreme pain, I'd prefer to avoid *Sadomasochistic Palace*," he said.

With a sigh of relief, Serena nodded. "I agree."

"Why don't you pick one, then I'll pick one, and if we both agree, we'll put it down for a daily activity?" he suggested.

"Good idea."

"You first."

Serena looked closely, that familiar shyness and uncertainty pounding like her rapidly beating heart. What if Michael laughed at her suggestion, or expressed shock at her choices? Well tough. She'd plunged head first into this adventure, and the time for hesitation was over.

"How about *Voyeurism Venture*?" she whispered, feeling silly for the heated blush that warmed her cheeks.

Michael smiled. "You like to watch?"

"I . . . I don't know. I've never watched before, but I think I'd like to."

"I'm game if you are," he said, his voice taking on a seductively husky edge that made her nipples tingle. God, what would happen when he actually touched her, when they got naked together? Would she self combust on the spot?

Now it was Michael's turn. "How about *Everything Oral*?"

Wetness formed between her legs the minute her mind registered exploring tongues, mouths and all forms of oral pleasures with the man sitting next to her. She moistened her lips with her tongue, and managed a squeaky, "Yes."

He smiled and wrote it on the form.

After the first couple, suggesting them became easier. It appeared Michael had no inhibitions, because every one of her choices met with his approval, and vice versa.

She was thrilled when his choice for their final day was the *Private Cove for Two*. That meant no props, groups, or other people. Just the two of them—a day filled with unbridled passion in a secluded spot for two. She couldn't wait.

Her body thrummed with anticipation. She knew she wouldn't sleep a wink tonight, imagining the activities laid out for the next several days.

This was the moment she'd waited for, the one she'd craved desperately. The chance to live out her fantasies with someone who appeared to be as eager to participate as she was.

Music started up in the background and Serena nursed her drink, her stomach fluttering nervously.

"Are you gonna be able to go through with all this?" Michael asked, leaning in to whisper in her ear. His breath sailed across her cheek, and she inhaled the sweet scent of fine whisky.

She nodded. "Yes, of course. I'm looking forward to it."

"Then I guess you wouldn't mind if we had a little taste of what's to come right now."

Mesmerized, she let him pull her to her feet. Right in front of everyone he slid his arms around her and pulled her to his chest. Her breasts crushed against the hard wall of muscle there. And it wasn't the only place a hard wall of muscle lived. His erection pressed against her thigh.

Oh, wow. He was built quite impressively. Thoughts of his long, hard cock sliding into her core danced through her imagination, vibrant images of hot sand, blistering sunlight and sweaty bodies moistening her, readying her. Oh hell, she'd been ready for hours already.

"You're breathing heavily," he said, coaxing her gaze to meet his by lifting her chin with his thumb. "You nervous?"

No point in hiding anything from him, since very shortly he'd know just how nervous she was. "A little. I've never done anything like this before."

He smiled, his full lips spreading wide. "Neither have I. But I'll tell you, my cock is raging hard right now, wondering if you're wearing panties under that dress."

Instantly she was a puddle of arousal. Her body quaked with the need to be touched, caressed. How long had it been since she'd had a decent orgasm? And at that, she'd done it herself.

Time for Sexy Siren Serena to surface.

"No panties," she whispered back in a throaty voice. "Would you like to explore a little?"

Chapter Three

🔊

Michael's eyes darkened at Serena's suggestion. His hand wound tighter around her waist, sliding lower to cup a handful of her buttocks. He pulled her against him, lightly rocking his erection against her dampening mound.

"Explore? Like this?" he asked.

She gasped as he reached under her dress, his rough fingers exploring the tender flesh of her inner thighs. He caressed her legs, his fingers barely millimeters away from the center of her pulsating heat.

"You're wet." His eyes held hers while he continued his torturous caress. "Here on your thighs, and I haven't even touched your pussy yet."

Serena focused on breathing. Whimpers of delight and need escaped her parted lips as Michael's questing fingers drew ever closer to her aroused flesh. She looked around at the other couples and singles. Some were in tune only to each other, their new conquests for the week, she supposed. A handful glanced in their direction, and smiled.

The fact they were being watched turned her on all the more.

A few inches more and his fingers would be on her clit. *Closer, just a little closer. Touch me, oh please touch me.* She bit her bottom lip to keep from begging him to hurry. Her pussy throbbed with anticipation. She already knew it would be good. She'd probably come right there on the dance floor, and wondered what kind of reaction she'd get from Michael if that happened. She was so close already, if he'd only move his fingers just an inch—

"I think we'll just leave it at anticipation for tonight," he said, withdrawing his hand from under the hem of her skirt.

Leave it? What was he talking about? She needed to be touched, and now, dammit!

Transfixed, she watched as he drew his fingers up to his nose, and inhaled.

"You smell like sweet sugar. I wonder if you taste as good as you smell?" He ran his index and middle fingers over his lips and licked them.

She couldn't help it. She moaned.

"Like honey," he said. "Does it excite you to watch me lick my fingers, knowing they're covered in your juices?"

She nodded, incapable of speech, barely able to stand. Her knees were jelly. She felt unsteady, wobbly, and was so damned turned on she wanted to scream in frustration.

"I'm going upstairs to do some work," he said. "Do me a favor."

"What?" She hoped he'd suggest she undress and lie down on his bed to wait for him, so he could finish what he'd started.

"Don't come tonight. Don't touch yourself. When you come, I want it to be with me. When it happens, I want to be there. I want to hear it, taste it, feel it."

Oh, man! Now that was asking a lot of her. Her body throbbed with need. It would only take a couple strokes and she'd be there. And now he was asking her to wait?

"I'll try."

The corners of his mouth lifted in an incredibly sexy smile. "You do that."

* * * * *

Don't come tonight. Serena grumbled remembering Michael's words of the night before. She cursed the morning sun streaming in through the open window of her bathroom.

She hadn't slept one bit last night, tossing and turning, her body heated to boiling with arousal, her thighs wet with her juices. And she'd told him she'd try. She had been close so many times during the night, thinking, *screw waiting – I need to come*. More than once her fingers had inched up her legs and she'd had to forcibly stop them from touching that sweet spot and sending her right over the edge.

But she hadn't. Because he was right. She wanted him to do it for her, wanted him to draw out the screaming orgasm she knew awaited her as soon as he touched her. What she should have done was march right into his room, climb on top of him and fit her aching, dripping pussy over his mouth and demand that he make her come.

He damn well better do it today, or she *would* be doing it herself. And she didn't care where or when it happened, as long as it happened.

After much deliberation she slipped on a sundress, this one as tight and revealing as the one she'd worn last night. Halter style and bright blue, it was cut low in the front, revealing a considerable amount of cleavage. Her breasts were half exposed on both sides. The hem barely skimmed the top of her thighs, and in fact, she was certain when she sat all her secrets would be revealed, since she purposely left her panties off. She piled her long hair on top of her head, securing it with a clip so that curled tendrils escaped. Satisfied, she set out to find Michael.

Let's see how long he holds out today. He'd rocked one hellacious erection against her last night. She knew he'd been as turned on as she was. Obviously, he possessed way more self-control than she did, or maybe he'd gotten off recently and hadn't needed it as badly as she had.

Either way, she was armed and ready for battle. Already itching to get Michael's hands, mouth and cock on her, she was prepared to do anything to make sure that happened. Before long she would touch him, taste him, feel his lips against her, rim the head of his engorged penis with her tongue.

A long time in the making, Serena's fantasies were going to come true.

She found him sitting at the table in front of the balcony, bathed in the morning sun. Engrossed in his work, he hadn't noticed her presence, which gave her a minute to drink her fill of him.

And what a drink it was. A tall drink—hot, dark and juicy. Full bodied, flavorful, a little taste of heaven. The kind you let slide slowly down your throat because you want to savor forever. She sighed contentedly, imagining looking at him every day for the next week. And not just looking, either, but running her fingers across the black curls liberally sprinkled across his well-toned chest and abdomen. Touching him everywhere. Tasting all of him. She wanted to jump into his lap, yank down his shorts, and ride his cock for a stiff morning workout.

"Good morning," she said, pleased that his eyes widened when he looked up at her.

"Morning. Sleep well?"

She caught the slight smirk of his upturned lips. "Not one bit. You?"

He shrugged. "Sleeping's overrated."

She laughed, sensing he'd been as frustrated as she. Somehow that made her feel a teeny bit better.

They ate breakfast downstairs in the lounge, then picked up their agenda at the front desk. Serena tore open the envelope, wondering if all their selections had been approved.

"We've got Voyeurism Venture today," she said with a tingle of excitement as she scanned the agenda. She looked up at him and smiled.

He arched a brow. "You ever watch people have sex before?"

"Not really."

"Not really? What does that mean?"

"I've only seen it in movies."

"Think it'll get you hot and bothered being in a room surrounded by people fucking?"

She didn't know if she'd actually enjoy it, but she'd thought about it for years. "I don't know, but that's why I'm here. To experience new things.

"Do you like watching porn?"

She nodded. "I have a library of videos."

"Mmm, we'll have to compare video titles."

She laughed at their discussion. She'd never be able to have this conversation with anyone in her small town. "The activity starts at three-thirty, so we have some time to kill."

Michael nodded. "I've got a bit more work to do, anyway. How about you?"

"I have a few things to occupy my time." Not really what she wanted to be doing, but if Michael had to work, she'd wait. For a little while longer, anyway.

They headed back to their suite and Michael went to work on his laptop. Serena picked up her college schedule and list of courses, figuring to do some planning for the next semester.

"What are you working on?" he asked.

"Lesson plans for fall."

"Subjects?"

"English lit, American lit, some freshman composition classes and creative writing."

"Really? Do you write?"

"Not on your life," she laughed. "I dissect what everyone else writes, and then work with some of the students to improve their writing skills." Putting the planner aside, she tucked her feet behind her on the couch. Michael's brows rose and he smiled appreciatively, obviously having caught a glimpse between her legs.

"Shaved, are you?"

Her libido, already raw and primed for action, jumped up a few more notches at the realization that he'd seen between her legs. And liked what he saw.

"Yes. Do you like it?"

"Hell, yeah. Besides being sexy as hell, it'll make it easier when I lick your pussy. Nothing in my way when I stroke my tongue along the soft folds of your bare skin."

She panted, her fingers once again itching to travel between her legs.

"Can you imagine that warm wetness gliding over you Serena? Hitting that sweet spot until you dig your hands in my hair and push my face against you, screaming for more?"

She swallowed. Hard. She was never going to make it until this afternoon. Not if he kept talking to her like that and looking at her like he wanted to eat her alive.

Right now, she wished he would. She'd gladly spread her legs and welcome his warm, wet tongue on her clit. She wanted to come so bad right now she could barely keep herself from sliding her hand down there and letting him watch her satisfy herself.

Maybe he'd enjoy that. A little prelude to today's activities. Then she'd get off and ease a little bit of the tension that had been building inside her for over twenty-four hours.

But instead he turned back to his work. Just like that. As if what he'd just said had no affect. Didn't he see how aroused she was?

Serena had to give him credit. He had a lot more willpower than she did.

* * * * *

Michael glanced down at the clock in the corner of his laptop screen, mentally counting the minutes. Might as well find something else to do since he sure as hell wasn't getting much work done.

He had to be insane. Completely, certifiably nuts. This foreplay game with Serena wasn't even enjoyable. His cock had been painfully hard since last night with no let up, and his balls were drawn tight, begging for release.

A release that couldn't come soon enough. Just watching Serena on the couch was torture. Her wiggling and shifting position every few minutes gave him a clear view of the most beautiful pussy he'd ever laid eyes on. He was dying to scoot her down on the couch until her ass lay over the edge, spread her legs and drive his tongue deep inside her honeyed folds, then let her return the favor and swallow his cock whole until he came buckets down her throat.

He should have jacked off last night, taken the edge off a bit. She'd gotten him hot damn fast. Hotter and faster than any woman ever had. His balls ached all night long as he rolled around in bed with a perpetual hard-on, imagining sliding between her silken thighs and taking what she'd so willingly offered. He'd wanted to bust down her door and tell her he wanted her, right then.

But he hadn't, remembering what he'd asked Serena to do, knowing how much he'd tortured her by asking her to wait before she came.

Torture was a dual-edged sword.

What a fucking moron he was. He could have taken care of both of them last night. Instead he ended up with blue balls.

He raked a hand through his hair and inhaled deeply, blowing it out slowly, hoping to gain some semblance of rational thought before he went totally off the deep end.

The only good thing about this whole situation was he now had a very clear picture of the incredibly beautiful and very seductive heroine for his next novel. She would be brilliant, with a penchant for the arts and a body that tantalized men to death and destruction. Just like Serena. A scholar's brain and a body that would surely kill him before the week was up.

They'd spent hours talking about her career, and his books. She wasn't lying when she'd told him she'd read his stuff. She knew his characters almost as well as he did.

And she had some damn good ideas about future plotlines. Serena was wicked sharp, able to process information within seconds and spit out facts, figures and dates. What she didn't know, she knew where to find.

When he'd asked her how she knew so much about crime and literature, she smiled and a cute little blush stained her cheeks. She'd explained there wasn't much night life in a small college town in Kansas, so she spent a lot of time reading and doing research.

What a surprising woman.

Thankfully the day passed quickly. It was time to leave for their adventure.

"You ready to go?" he asked, his penis standing up and taking the lead.

"More than ready," she mumbled. He sensed her frustration. Good. The anticipation would make the release that much sweeter.

They wound their way through the garden paths towards their destination. Serena seemed fascinated by the tropical plants and flowers, stopping every few feet to read the signs proclaiming their rarity.

Unfortunately, every time she bent over to read a placard, Michael's cock strained toward her like a dog barely on the leash. The skimpy dress rode up her thighs, exposing the cheeks of her fabulous ass and that sweet shaved slit that he wanted to bury both his tongue and cock inside. As secluded as the garden areas were, it would be easy to nestle up behind her, lift her dress up and plunge into her heat.

And he'd bet she wouldn't complain one bit, either. From her inability to sit still to her half-dilated eyes and hard nipples, he knew if he made the suggestion right now she'd eagerly bend over for him.

But that wasn't the way he wanted this to play out. Stupid, he knew, but he had a plan. Try as he might to ignore Serena as a person, he couldn't. And she seemed, despite her bravado, more or less inexperienced. Not that she didn't have fantasies— it was obvious that she had a vivid imagination. But if he took things too quickly, it wouldn't be as good for her as he knew it could be.

Why in the hell did he care? He never had before, certainly not with Ginny or any of the other women who came before her. He hadn't cared since Mari. And he wasn't going down that road again.

Ah, hell, what did it matter? Not much longer, and they'd both scratch the almost unbearable itch for each other. For the time being, he'd chalk it all up to research.

They arrived at Voyeur's Bungalow, a one-story ranch house. Michael followed Serena through the front door, watching her reaction. Her eyes widened at the theater type atmosphere. Everything from loveseats to sex swings to a standing area in the back was available. Even some chaise lounges where he bet there'd be some action before the event was over.

In front of the massive seating area was a stage of sorts. Nothing more than a bare room with dark brocade draperies and wall hangings, and silken pillows and blankets. Sex swings suspended from the ceiling were interspersed among the bedding.

Anticipation roared through Michael's body, his cock already twitching with excitement. This should be fun.

"You want to sit or stand?" he asked, stepping up behind Serena and laying his hands on her bare shoulders. Her fragrance wafted toward him and he breathed in the sweet scent of gardenia and musky woman. He couldn't resist trailing a finger down her beautiful neck, watching over her shoulder as her nipples hardened and pressed against the flimsy silk of her dress.

"Stand," she murmured, her eyes not once leaving the stage as couples began to assemble there.

Michael stayed behind and a little to her left so he could watch her face. Her eyes widened and her breathing increased as the participants began to kiss and fondle each other.

The lights lowered to a candlelight illumination—bright enough to see, but more sensuous than the glaring chandeliers above. A slow, sexy jazz rhythm emanated from the speakers in the corners of the room.

There were multiple pairings, both heterosexual as well as gay and lesbian. Every voyeur's delight – a smorgasbord of erotic viewing. Clearly this event served more than one purpose. Eye candy for the voyeurs, and heightened sexual pleasure for the exhibitionists on the stage.

It didn't take long for the action to start. Clothes were quickly disposed of, kissing became groping. The sounds of moans and gasps increased as the foreplay built. The sounds and smells filled the room. Writhing bodies found beds and swings, mouths found cocks and pussies and the scent of sex was everywhere.

Michael had to admit it was a considerable turn on to watch other people fuck. His cock begged for release from his shorts. He pressed his erection against Serena's full, round ass, rewarded by her swift moan of pleasure. She backed against him and swiveled her hips from side to side, reaching behind her to clutch his upper thighs and hold his erection firmly in place between the cheeks of her ass.

Resting his head against hers he reached around and searched out the gorgeous breasts he'd been dying to touch. He slid his hands into the gaps in the side of her dress and breathed deeply as his hands found the ample globes. His thumbs grazed her nipples and she jerked against him.

Not once had she taken her eyes off the activities on the stage. Michael spared a glance at the action in front of him. One couple was in a sixty-nine position, the woman on her back taking all of the man's erection into her willing mouth. His head was buried between her legs, her hips bucking off the floor as she ground her pussy against his mouth.

Another couple had taken a position behind a high backed chair. The woman bent over at the waist and held onto the chair while the man pounded his lengthy shaft into her.

Michael spied an interesting three-way. A gorgeous, dark haired woman sat on the chaise, one leg draped over a man on either side of her, her pussy wide open for their questing fingers. She had a cock in each hand, stroking furiously.

Serena hadn't uttered a word, but he heard her rapid breaths.

"Do you like what you see?" he whispered against her ear, following up his question with a light lick of her earlobe.

"Yes," she managed in a raspy voice. "Oh, yes."

"Do you like me touching your breasts like this?"

"Oh God, yes. Pinch my nipples, Michael."

He growled in her ear and took each nipple between his thumb and forefinger, rolling lightly. She gasped and ground her ass into his straining cock.

If she kept that up he'd be coming in his shorts. And that's not the way he planned this day. When he came, it was either going to be in her pussy, her mouth, or all over those gorgeous breasts of hers.

Even the voyeurs had gotten into the action. Couples all around them were fucking, sucking and groping. It looked like an orgy—he couldn't tell where one group stopped and another began. Nor did he think the participants cared.

"Look at the people around us, Serena."

She slowly turned her focus away from the stage. The woman next to them was spread out on a chaise. Her t-shirt had been pulled above her full breasts, and she was naked from the waist down. A sweating, straining man had his shaft buried deep within her. He thrust and withdrew, the distended veins of his hard, wet cock visible.

Serena whimpered and sucked in her bottom lip. Michael desperately wanted those full lips wrapped around his cock. He wanted everything, and he wanted it right now.

Slow down. Breathe. Make this good for both of you.

"Tell me what you want, Serena. What are you feeling?"

Her breasts rose and fell in his hands as she panted her response. "I . . . Oh God, Michael. I need to come, and I need to come right now."

Chapter Four

ഇ

I need to come right now. Holy shit, she was getting bold. Or desperate. Or both. Serena couldn't believe she'd just told Michael she needed an orgasm. Actually it was more than that—she'd demanded one. But, dammit, she *did* need one. Her body shuddered, begging for release. The visuals all around her excited her more than she ever expected. Michael's hands on her only added to her already near-frenzied anticipation.

She could care less if he threw her to the ground and fucked her right there. In fact, she'd welcome it with open legs.

"You need to come? Right now? Right here? With all these people around you?" he teased, his ragged voice rough against her ear.

"Yes," she managed through rapid breaths. "Right here. I don't care. I want it now!"

She heard his husky laugh, felt his cock pressing urgently against her ass, and knew he wanted it as much as she did.

"Tell me," he said, moving to her side and running his hands over the swell of her hip, then lower. "Tell me which one of the scenes you're watching turns you on the most?"

What scenes? That would require thought. How could she think when his hands were edging ever closer to that pulsating spot between her legs? Her juices seeped down her thigh and she throbbed with an ache that threatened to drop her to her knees. Now she had to think?

Turning her gaze to the stage, she scanned the participants and made her choice. The one her eyes kept coming back to, time and time again.

"The woman stroking the two guys," she managed between gasps. Michael's fingers burned against the skin of her upper thigh. He slowly began to raise the hem of her dress. Her heat level rose with every centimeter.

"Why?" he whispered, pressing his erection against her hip, thrusting it against her like she was dying for him to thrust inside her. Hard, relentless, just like she wanted him to fuck her.

What was it about the scene that struck her? The fact a woman serviced two men, or that the woman seemed to be enjoying it so much? The woman's eyes were near closed, her mouth open, and she periodically licked her lips as if she really wanted to wrap her mouth around one of the cocks she stroked.

"I've never seen anything like that before. It's so erotic."

"You like stroking a man's cock, Serena?"

"Yes . . . Oh God, yes." She wasn't certain if her response pertained more to the fantasy come to life in front of her, or that Michael's fingers were bare inches from her clit.

"Would you like to stroke two guys at the same time?"

"I . . . I don't know." How could she think when his touch turned her body to liquid, flaming lava? "Oh yes, Michael, there. Touch me there."

His fingers found the magic spot. Hell, her entire body was a magic spot right now. The incredible sensation of his hands searching through her wet folds almost sent her over the edge. But she held off, wanting to prolong the pure ecstasy of finally having Michael's hands on her.

A ragged moan escaped her lips and he murmured in her ear. "You're so wet, Serena. You like my fingers gliding over your clit and your slick, wet pussy, don't you?"

She arched her back against him in response, pushing her mound against his fingers. His thumb stroked her clit like a violin—back and forth he played her, just the right rhythm to

45

heighten the intensity level. He knew just how to touch her, shooting off sparks of pleasure that reverberated through her.

He kept one hand on her breast—fondling, tweaking the nipple, which sent shocks of desire straight down to the ache between her legs. It wasn't going to take much longer, she knew it. And yet she wanted to hold back, wanted to savor the moment. It had been so long since a man had touched her. And no man had *ever* touched her like this.

When he slipped two fingers between the folds of her lips and inserted them inside her, she whimpered long and low. "Oh, God, you're going to make me come."

"Come on baby," he whispered, his fingers sliding slowly in and out, his thumb drawing torturous circles against her clit. "Come for me."

She tilted her head back against his shoulder, pushed her mound against his hand and screamed out with a shattering orgasm. Spasms racked her body and she shuddered as shock after shock of piercing pleasure arced through her.

It seemed to last forever, and was over way too soon. Gasping for breath, trying to regain some semblance of normalcy was nearly impossible. Michael breathed deeply against her, ruffling the hair against the side of her face.

"That was nice, babe," he whispered, continuing to stroke her slit. "Very nice. My hand is soaked with your come."

She'd felt it, the gushing fluid pouring out of her as her pussy clamped down around his fingers. Never had she had an orgasm like that—never. Not even the ones she'd given herself were that intense, and she knew her own body better than any man ever could.

At least she thought she had. Now, she wasn't sure. Michael had instinctively known exactly where to touch her, concentrating his strokes on areas that pleasured her the most. She hadn't even had to guide his hand to her sweet spot. He'd known right where to go.

And now, it was his turn.

She turned to face him, winding her arms around his neck.

"Thank you," she whispered, nestling close against him, his cock straining against her pelvis.

"You're welcome." His eyes were dark blue pools. His breathing was shallow, his shoulders rising and falling with every fevered breath.

"I'm going to make you come now, Michael."

He sucked in a breath. "Do it. I need it after touching you, listening to you, feeling your pussy clench and gush all over my hand."

He needed her. Could one person handle this much pleasure?

Watching the scenes before her, both onstage and in the voyeur area, had taken her sexual excitement to a new peak. She wanted to experience everything she'd watched. Wanted Michael's penis in her hands, wanted to taste the drops of come that would drip from the tip once she circled her lips around him.

Her eyes never leaving his face, she dropped to her knees before him.

He shuddered a breath and looked down.

With two hands she grasped the sides of his shorts and pulled them down over his hips and thighs.

He wore no underwear, either. His erection sprang out in front of her. Huge, hard, almost as if it had a mind of its own and searching for her.

"Wow."

With a laugh, Michael said, "You like it?"

"Oh yeah." He was built quite well. Had to be at least eight inches, thick and nicely shaped. Even tilted upward a little, guaranteeing he'd hit her G-spot when he fucked her. The thought of that big cock filling her had her licking her lips in anticipation. Which wasn't the only thing she wanted to do with her lips. She could already imagine wrapping her mouth around the ridged edge of his shaft and sucking him in.

Without hesitation she took his cock in her hand and was immediately rewarded with a guttural groan from Michael. His heat pulsed against her palm.

"Feels like I've been waiting years for you to get your hands on my cock."

"I know. I feel the same way. If I'd have known what I was missing, I'd have gotten to it first thing yesterday."

"Well, it's yours now, baby. Get to it."

Turning the tables on him, she hesitated, her gaze riveted on his. "Tell me what you see that turns you on the most."

He smiled darkly at her. "That's easy. The couple standing up. She's leaning over the chair, he's fucking her from behind."

"You like that?" she asked, using both her hands to stroke him, gently but firmly, his shaft pulsing with energy.

"Oh yeah. I like that. I'm gonna fuck you that way this week."

The image of his thick cock slamming into her from behind made her shiver. She felt the damp spurts of arousal between her legs, her body awakening again. "Oh, I hope so."

"You have great hands," he said, watching her every move.

Serena was shocked at their erotic play. She'd never been so brazen, so willing to experiment right out in the open with people watching. He made her forget the other people, made her forget everything but him. She'd even screamed out her orgasm with all these people around her, and hadn't cared one damn bit. And now she had Michael's huge shaft in her hands. She slid her thumb over the tip, rewarded when a bead of moisture seeped from its head and spilled over onto her finger. She slipped her finger in her mouth and moaned at the sheer pleasure of tasting him.

He growled low and long, watching her.

"You taste great, Michael. Salty and sweet." She leaned in to take him into her mouth, but he stopped her.

"Save that," he rasped. "I want something else."

"What?"

"Undo the top of your dress. I want to see your breasts."

Her nipples puckered and came to life as if they'd heard his words. She undid the button at her neck and slid the halter down until it rested at her waist.

His eyes lit up and his lips curved into a smile. "You have gorgeous breasts."

She ached for his touch, his mouth, his tongue on her engorged nipples. She could barely balance on her haunches with the way he was looking at her.

"Stroke my cock. I want to come on your breasts."

Serena settled back on her knees, excited beyond words at Michael's suggestion. She'd get to watch. Watch his shaft grow and harden, pulsate in her hand until he shot his load all over her breasts. Another first for her. Everything with him had been a first, and an unexpected glimpse into her own fantasies.

She wanted everything with him. Starting with this.

"That's it," he murmured, guiding her as she stroked the length of him. "Nice and slow. Now squeeze a little harder, I want it to feel like my cock is in your tight pussy. "

Gripping him firmly, she slid her enclosed hands from the tip of his penis to the base, reveling in his sounds of pleasure. Keeping one hand on his shaft, her motions constant, she slid the other underneath and cupped his balls.

Michael bucked against her, driving his cock harder and faster into her hand. She squeezed his balls lightly while maintaining the rhythmic stroking.

"Oh, yeah, like that," he said.

Despite her position on her knees in front of him, Serena felt empowered. She controlled his cock with her hands, controlled the amount of pleasure she gave him. He was totally and completely at her mercy, and she was relentless in her desire to please him.

Like the woman who'd jacked off those two men, she was in charge. Judging from the sweat glistening over Michael's stomach and legs and the distended veins running over the surface of his cock, she was doing a pretty damn good job.

The head of his penis colored a deep purple as he forced his length through her eager hands. From his increased movements, she could sense he was getting close. Feeling a near triumphant satisfaction, she stepped up her efforts, closing the circle her hands provided, making him work harder to penetrate the tight hold she had on him, squeezing him until he groaned long and low.

"Shit. Oh fuck, baby, yeah. Like that. Faster. I can't hold off much longer."

His voice rasped as he thrust harder against her. She leaned back so that he could watch. With one long shout of ecstasy he shot a hot stream of come all over her breasts, his cock pulsing against her hand.

It was the most erotic experience she'd ever had. Listening to him, feeling him, knowing she'd been responsible for giving him this pleasure, made her body ache for more.

She kept up her strokes, slowly, gently, until she'd milked every last drop of come from him. Then she sat back, supremely pleased with herself and smiled up at him.

Michael blew out a breath, pulled up his shorts and grabbed a towel. He lifted her to a standing position and wiped her breasts, sliding the towel over her distended nipples until she was breathing hard again.

"Thank you," he said after she'd refastened her halter.

"You're welcome."

Finally focusing again on the people around her, most were in the aftereffects of their own orgasms. How had she missed it all? She'd been so occupied with Michael she hadn't once stopped to look at the action around her.

Apparently, at least for her, the voyeurism was exciting only to the point where she focused on the man with her. After that, she'd tuned them out completely.

Couples had begun to depart. She and Michael followed, heading back to their room. A comfortable silence accompanied their walk through the gardens. Serena wondered what he was thinking, but despite the intimacy they'd just shared, she didn't feel right asking.

"I'm going to take a shower," he said as soon as they entered the suite.

She went to do the same, stepping into to her own bedroom to clean up. As the water sprayed over her body, Serena recalled every erotic moment of today's adventure. The event had exceeded her wildest expectations. She'd even surprised herself. Thinking she'd be shy at first, once they'd gotten started and she watched everyone around her going at it, engaging in sexual play right there with Michael seemed as natural as breathing.

Was it the location, was it her, or was it her partner? She was comfortable with Michael. He encouraged her fantasies, not once turning down anything she suggested. He was perfect.

Whoa. Not perfect. Just for the week. Just for sex. She had to keep reminding herself that this was temporary. She had no relationship with Michael other than as a sexual partner. To think otherwise would be disastrous. When this week was over, they'd go their separate ways, and the only thing she'd be taking back to Kansas with her would be memories.

After slipping on a pair of shorts and a tube top, Serena came out of the bedroom to find Michael. He was on the couch, his hair still damp from his shower. As she was finding typical, he wore only navy shorts and no shirt.

He turned when she came in, and smiled at her. "Nice outfit," he said, eyeing her from head to toe appreciatively.

"Thanks." She warmed under his gaze and took a seat on the couch. Not close like they were earlier, somehow she felt it would be presumptuous to cuddle up next to him.

"You sure dress differently than when you first got here."

"Those were my 'Kansas college professor' clothes," she explained before looking down at the tight shorts and matching black tube top that barely contained her breasts. "This is my vacation wear."

He laughed. "I see. Not much call for skimpy, sexy little outfits where you live, huh?"

"Hardly."

"You should try southern California sometime. It's the dressing norm."

Ah, so that was where he lived? "I've never been to California."

"It's nice. Kind of like this, only not so tropical."

California sounded wonderful. And free.

"You hungry?" he asked.

"Starving."

"Want to see what's in the fridge?"

She nodded and they headed into the kitchen together.

Each suite came with a fully stocked kitchen. They decided on an omelet, which Michael offered to fix. She chopped the mushrooms and ham while he prepared the egg mixture, then dumped in the meat and vegetables and some shredded cheese. Serena heard her stomach grumble. Michael must have, too.

"I know," he said. "Sex works up an appetite, doesn't it?"

Sex. Now the subject was out in the open. "Yes, it would seem so."

"Don't you get hungry after sex?"

With her back to him as she poured juice into glasses and pulled out dishes and utensils, she shrugged. "I really wouldn't know. I haven't had that much sex in my lifetime."

She turned to him, plates in hand, as he shifted the omelets from the pan to the plates. They walked out onto the balcony to eat and watch the sun set over the ocean.

The omelets were delicious. The man could even cook, wonder of wonders. Was there anything he couldn't do?

"What did you mean, you haven't had much sex?" he asked in between mouthfuls.

Serena swallowed and took a drink of juice. "Well, not much good sex, anyway."

He laughed. "Then they didn't do it right."

"Don't I know it."

"Just how experienced are you?" he asked.

"I've had a few relationships. Not much, and certainly not the kind I can experience here."

"Why not?"

"Well, I worked my way through college, all the way to getting my PhD. Wasn't much time for the typical college relationships. Plus, I stayed close to home."

"What? They don't have guys in your town?" he teased.

She laughed. "Yeah, they do, but it wasn't like I was going to tell any of the guys I had sex with that I had all these kinky ideas and wanted to explore them."

"Why wouldn't you?"

She shrugged. "Afraid, I guess."

"Of?"

"Small towns are notoriously incestuous. Everyone knows everyone. And knows what everyone is doing, and with whom. I knew I'd want to stay there to teach, and all it would have taken was one guy to spout off about my unusual fantasies and it would have been all over town."

He quirked a brow. "You don't give guys much credit."

"Correction. I didn't give the guys I'd slept with much credit. And anyway, I was too busy for an active sex life, so there were only a few."

"A few isn't a lot, is it?" he asked.

She sighed. "Not nearly enough."

"Is that why you're here? Because you wanted more in depth experience?"

She pushed her now empty plate to the side. "I guess so. I don't know, really. It's not like there are a ton of guys I could indulge my fantasies with in the tiny town where I live. Reputation and all."

He nodded. "Not seemly for a college professor to be seen cavorting at nudist camps and swingers parties, huh?"

She snorted a laugh. "I'd lose my job, and everything I've worked for."

"Why don't you move to a larger city? Where you could be a little more anonymous?"

"Roots, I guess. I grew up not far from there, so I just stayed in my own back yard."

"You have family nearby?"

She shook her head. "Not anymore. My parents are both dead and I have no other relatives."

"I'm sorry." He laid his hand over hers.

"Thank you. It was a long time ago, when I was barely out of high school. Stupid car crash on icy roads." All these years and still the pain of their loss clenched at her heart.

"How long ago?" he asked, obviously curious about her age.

"I'm twenty-eight, if that's what you're asking."

He didn't say anything, so she asked. "How old are you, Michael?"

"I'm thirty-three."

She'd guessed right.

"Must have been tough for you, trying to go to college and having no support."

"I managed."

"Is that what you're doing now, Serena? Just managing?"

She met his gaze. The concern etched on his features made her uncomfortable. His questions made her uncomfortable. She wasn't there to delve into anything but the sexual things lacking in her life. "I don't know. I guess."

"Managing isn't the same as living, you know. You've got a vibrancy, a natural zest for life and excitement that you're obviously not fulfilling in that dinky little hovel you live in. Vacations like this are fun and all, but eventually you have to go home."

"I'm doing fine," she asserted, not wanting to think about her real life during this week of adventure.

"Fine. Managing. This is fantasy, Serena. When you get back home next week, you'll be living. Or, should I say, 'managing.' It's not good enough. A woman like you shouldn't wither away in an unfulfilling existence. You need a different life."

She stood, intending to gather the plates and wash the dishes. Running, that's what she was doing. Running away from thoughts of how miserable her life was. She didn't need this, not right now, not when she'd just started to have fun.

Michael stopped her, his hand grasping her wrist before she could pile the plates in her arms. "Don't run away. Talk about this."

"Why?" she asked. "Why do you care about me? What we have together is only a week of fun and games. Nothing more. When it's over, you'll go back to California and I'll go back to Kansas, and that's the end. My personal life is none of your business."

His eyes narrowed, his jaw clenched. Anger and something else—frustration, maybe, etched his face. "Maybe not. But this week you're my business. And my pleasure."

He pulled her towards him and crushed his mouth to hers.

Chapter Five

ഔ

Serena's toes curled. She welcomed this first kiss with Michael like she'd been starving for his mouth. Despite her irritation at his questions about her boring life, she wanted, needed his lips on hers. Those full, sensuous lips, that mouth she'd ached to taste since they'd first met.

He tasted like hot sex in the summer. Juice clung to his lips and she licked it off. His tongue swept into her mouth and grabbed for hers, twining and undulating like the magical dance of sex. Moisture pooled between her legs as his sensuous lips caressed hers. She knew then, knew that what she'd experienced earlier today, had only been a prelude to what would happen later.

She wrapped her arms around his neck, clinging to him, pressing against his hardening shaft, knowing as well as he did that they had unfinished business. They had so much more to share.

Tearing his mouth away, he rained kisses down her throat, stopping to take a little nibble out of that spot where her neck met her shoulder. She shivered, delighting in the scrape of his teeth against her flesh.

His skin felt heated to her touch. She slipped her hands over his broad shoulders, then over his chest, tangling her fingernails into the crisp hairs, searching and finding his nipples. She flicked her thumbs over the flat nubs, feeling them bud to life.

Michael inhaled sharply.

"You like having your nipples touched," she whispered, pulling back to gaze into his darkening eyes.

"Yes," he rasped. "So do you." With one yank he pulled her tube top down, exposing her breasts and gathering them in his hands.

Michael drank in the sight of her breasts, feeling the weight of them with his hands. She was perfectly proportioned, curvy in all the right places. He didn't have to worry about breaking her if he held her too tight. Huge breasts and lush hips, a woman made for a man. His erection made its presence known, jutting up between them.

He pulled at her round, pink nipples until they distended like ripe strawberries. He ached to fit his mouth around them and suck them, wanted to draw them out with his lips, hear her gasp with pleasure like she'd done earlier today.

Her orgasm had ripped through him earlier, taking him on the same wild ride. Never before had he seen a woman let go so completely. She'd been completely immersed in the sensations at the voyeur room today, soaking in the sights and sounds of the erotic escapades before them. And wanted—no—demanded that she have her share.

What an amazing woman. And how easy it would be to get caught up with her, to want more than just a week of casual sex.

But that wasn't going to happen. Michael knew that. They had different lives in the real world. And he was a cynic, finished with any notion of love. Fucking was fine. Love was a dream—a forgotten fantasy. At least for him.

Serena needed to find a man to love her. Someone who would give her everything she craved.

He focused on her now, watching her green eyes darken with passion. Her mouth opened, those full lips begging for his kiss. Her breathing quickened every time he rubbed his palms over her swollen nipples.

What he wanted to do was sweep her up into his arms, carry her to his bed and fuck her all night long until this strange need for her went away.

But that wasn't what he was going to do. Taking her to his bed would be intimate, personal. Best to keep things between them the way he originally intended.

Fun and games, and fucking. And only at the events they'd scheduled for the week. Nothing more.

He dropped his hands to his sides, ignoring the stab of guilt he felt at the confused look on her face. Dragging his fingers through his hair, he said, "I've got some work to do. Think I'll go take some quiet time in my room and start on my plot outline."

Her bottom lip trembled, and she sucked it in. Probably so he wouldn't see her disappointment. Fuck. Now he felt like an asshole.

Well, why not? He *was* an asshole.

"Did you want to bounce some story ideas off me?" she asked, pulling her top up over her breasts.

"Nah, not right now. I'm beat, and not fit company for other humans."

"Did I do something to offend you?" she asked.

Shit. Now he really felt like a prick. "No. Not at all. I just don't want to start something I'll be too tired to finish." Yeah right. Like he'd ever be too tired to get naked with Serena.

"Oh. All right, then. I'm kind of tired myself. Think I'll head to my room and work for awhile."

"Good night."

He watched her walk away, knowing he'd hurt her feelings. He felt like kicking himself. Nothing like teasing the woman to a frenzied state of arousal and then dumping her on her ass.

Nice move, Donovan. Real nice move.

* * * * *

Serena stood in the bathroom, irritated that she'd spent another sleepless night punching her pillow. She'd stared at the moon, its smiling craters mocking her, until the morning sun peeked in and she realized how fruitless attempts at sleep were.

She was such an idiot. What did she think was going to happen between them last night? That Michael would carry her to his bed and make love to her?

That wasn't what this week was about. It was about sex. Fucking, to be exact. Living out her fantasies. Not some dreamy, emotional involvement leading to romance.

When would she learn? For a year she'd planned this trip, looking forward to some impersonal, unemotional sex. And what had she found so far?

Nothing.

Except Michael. Hot, sexy, witty, adventurous Michael.

With a flick of her wrist the hairbrush went sailing across the bathroom counter, skidding to a halt at the very edge.

That's how she felt. On the edge. Itchy. Like she had a rash and desperately wanted to scratch it.

Sex. That's what she needed. What they'd done yesterday just whet her appetite for what could be. That's what she'd focus on today. Keep things impersonal between her and Michael. He was a mouth, hands and a penis. That's all. There to give her pleasure, and nothing more.

Figuring on spending the day by the pool, she threw on her skimpiest bikini and a see through cover up, slipped into her sandals, and tossed her unruly hair into a clip.

With a renewed resolve to toughen up, she threw open the door of the bedroom and sought him out.

There he was again, just like the day before—bare-chested, wearing shorts, and reading the paper out on the balcony. She sighed and grabbed a cup of coffee, poured in a touch of cream and flounced outside, determined to be cool, casual and unaffected.

"Morning," she said brightly.

He dropped one side of the paper and peered up at her warily. "Mornin'."

"Sleep well?" She sat and picked up a section of the newspaper, all but ignoring him.

"Fine," he grumbled.

She smiled behind the newspaper. Evidently he didn't sleep either.

"I slept like the dead. As soon as I went to my room I laid down and, boom, that was it."

"How nice for you."

Suppressing a giggle, she sipped her coffee silently.

"What's on tap for today?" he asked.

"*Everything Oral,*" she stated matter-of-factly, despite the tingling between her legs at the thought of getting her mouth on that fine cock of his.

He didn't respond. Just grumbled.

"Feel like begging off?" she asked.

He pulled the paper away from her face, his mouth set in a grim line. "You got someone else picked out to suck on today?"

Men were so dense sometimes. "No. Just didn't want to force you to participate if you didn't want to."

"I can participate just fine."

"Fine, then."

"Fine."

That went well. He sure had a bug up his ass this morning. Cranky from lack of sleep, or regrets that he'd gotten involved in these escapades with her in the first place?

Yesterday he'd seemed fine about the whole thing, eager even. And he'd clearly enjoyed the Voyeurism Venture.

Last night, he'd been the one to initiate that kiss and what followed, and he'd been the one to stop it abruptly. So whatever bothered him, it was about him, not her. She wasn't going to spend another minute of time worrying about what crawled up his ass. When the time came for them to play, they'd play. When it was over, they'd go their separate ways.

Safer for both of them that way.

"I'm going to grab some fruit and head out to the beach until it's time for our event."

He dropped the newspaper into his lap and stared at her as if he were looking at her for the first time. His gaze roamed over her body, making her feel naked.

She liked that feeling. Liked knowing that the two little triangles barely covered her breasts, and the thong bottom had little more than a scrap to cover her mound.

What she liked most was the way his eyes darkened and his breathing stilted.

It seemed as if he wanted to say something, but then he closed his mouth. "Have fun."

"I'll be back later." He didn't respond, so she grabbed her beach bag and headed out the door.

The beach was gorgeous. Pale sand and comfortable lounge chairs littered the pool area, just steps away from the turquoise ocean. Serena breathed in the salty sea spray and the sweet tropical flowers and smiled up at the warming sun.

The resort was completely secluded, the only habitated place on the island. Other than the various buildings, the entire place was completely private.

She spread her blanket over the cushioned chaise and lathered lotion on her body, then untied her halter strings so she wouldn't get tan lines. Not that there was much to the material, anyway. As it was, she should just tan naked. Most of the other guests were.

And some of them had seen her all but naked yesterday. So why did it matter?

Midwestern values, she supposed. And body image, like most women. She was no fashion model, that was for certain.

She was simply—average. Some things she could get past, others would obviously take some time, if ever, to put by the wayside.

The sun relaxed her and after awhile she shifted over onto her stomach, feeling drowsy. Before long she felt herself drifting off. She didn't know how long she'd been out, but a voice brought her around.

"Serena."

She lifted her head and saw Michael sitting in the chaise next to her.

"How long have you been sitting there?" she asked, stifling a yawn.

"About a half hour. You were out cold."

She stretched to clear the sleep cobwebs from her head, retied her halter, then turned around and lifted the chair to a sitting position.

He'd brought her a glass of iced tea. "Thanks," she murmured, taking a giant swallow. The sun was hot today, and the cool liquid sliding down her throat was a welcome relief.

Something else sliding down her throat later would be even better, she thought, eyeing Michael.

"Want to take a dip in the ocean?" he asked, putting the book in his lap on the table between them.

"Sure." A splash of cold water was exactly what she needed to bring her to a fully awake mindset. Although thinking about sucking his cock sure woke up certain parts of her quickly.

He rose and held out his hand for her. She looked at him, warmed by the first genuine smile she'd seen on his face all day. Maybe they'd both been grumpy and simply needed some distance. She definitely felt better after a little nap.

The water was cool, but not unpleasant. They waded in, hand in hand before Michael let go and dove under the surf. Serena stood in the water, waiting for him to surface.

He didn't. She turned around, feeling suddenly nervous, when suddenly she felt a tug on her ankle and she slipped under the water. She surfaced quickly—sputtering and spitting water out of her mouth. When she cleared her eyes of the stinging salt spray, she saw Michael treading in front of her, a boyish grin on his face.

"Jerk," she said, but couldn't hold back the smile.

"Couldn't help it," he said. "You were an easy target."

They swam out a distance to a floating dock and jumped out to sit and catch their breath, leaving their feet dangling in the water.

Being with Michael felt nice. Perfect. They sat comfortably together, their hips and shoulders touching.

"I was grouchy this morning. Sorry," he finally said.

"Me too. Don't worry about it. Neither of us has gotten much sleep since we got here."

He arched a brow. "I thought you said you went right to sleep last night."

She felt her face heat, and knew it wasn't from the sun. "I lied."

He laughed and pushed her wet hair out of her eyes. His gaze lingered, as did his hand against her cheek.

Please, please kiss me. She needed to feel that closeness with him, that bonding of lips against lips, the most intimate of the sexual acts they'd share this week. His mouth was heaven…soft and romantic, leaving her breathless with desire. *Bring me to life, Michael. I only have one week. I need you.*

She didn't care that it meant nothing, that it wouldn't be personal or romantic. She simply needed it.

He must have read her mind, because he cupped his hand behind her neck and pulled her face towards his, pressing a salty kiss to her lips. She sighed and breathed in the scent of him, so masculine and powerful like the sea surrounding her. His tongue lightly tangled with hers and her mind drifted to an image of the two of them on the dock, stripped naked with him poised above her, driving his big cock between her wide spread legs.

They could go at it right here, right now, and no one would think anything of it. But then again, it wouldn't be within the confines of their scheduled activities, and that's where their sex games should stay.

More impersonal that way. She couldn't help the desire to get more personal with him right now.

"It's almost time," he whispered after he pulled back from the kiss.

His voice broke the spell of fantasy she weaved, brought her back to the reality of being with him again — intimately, erotically. "I know."

"I've wanted to taste you. Been thinking about it a lot."

Visions of their bodies entangled, their mouths sucking and licking anywhere and everywhere they desired, flew through her mind. "I've wanted to suck your cock, Michael. I want that sweet taste of you in my mouth again. You know I only had a slight little flavor of you cross my lips yesterday."

"Yes, same for me. That one little taste of your sweet pussy left me hungry for more. I'm going to make you come today, Serena, with my tongue. Over and over and over again."

She sucked in a breath, suddenly unable to think about anything except the promise in Michael's deep blue eyes.

His gaze swept over her body — everywhere his eyes touched a caress against her heated skin. "You ready?"

She nodded, and they swam back to shore. Serena raced upstairs and jumped in the shower. She dried her hair, put on a little makeup, then chose her outfit for the adventure.

She smiled, thinking about Michael undressing her, revealing her skin bit by bit, his mouth licking and biting every part of her. And then she'd do the same to him. Dampness pooled between her thighs and her libido fired up hot and ready.

Purposely leaving her panties off, she slipped on the black spandex micro mini skirt, knowing it barely covered her ass cheeks. Next she chose a tiger striped tank top that laced in the front. Near transparent, it stretched and clung to her breasts, accentuating her aroused nipples.

Thank technology for Internet shopping, she thought. She'd never have found skimpy, sexy little clothes like these at her local shopping mall.

Slipping on high heeled sandals that made her appear as if she were all legs, she took a glance in the full length mirror and didn't recognize the woman standing before her.

Gone was Dr. Serena Graham, Professor of Literature. In her place stood Sexy Siren Serena, armed and ready for Oral Adventures.

She was going to blow Michael's mind today, among other things. With a light hearted giggle she went in search of her prey.

Chapter Six

Michael followed behind Serena, watching that fiery ass of hers sway back and forth underneath the tight little skirt. With every step he caught a glimpse of the bottom of her ass.

Fuck. She could make him go from zero to hard in an instant.

When she'd stepped out of the bedroom he had to fight to keep from drooling. The skimpy little skirt and tight, tiger striped shirt that barely held her breasts in was pure torture.

His throat went dry and his cock sprang to attention. Painful, aching attention. Like it had been for the past three days.

At least he'd get some relief now.

This time the adventure room was private. Much smaller than the voyeur theater, the small bedroom contained a king sized bed and a round, whirlpool tub. Huge windows surrounded the entire room. On the second floor, the windows would allow light in and a chance to see the island around them, still affording them all the privacy they'd want.

For those who wanted privacy, anyway. Some guests opted for the first floor room for their oral play, not minding a bit if others walked by and peeked in.

But Michael wanted privacy, wanted Serena to himself today. The group stuff yesterday had been fun. Now it was time for some one-on-one action.

With mouths and tongues.

He shifted, his hard-on pressing insistently against his shorts, begging for release. It couldn't come soon enough.

If this was what the hero in his next book would have to endure, the poor guy might be begging for death by chapter three.

Serena smiled and turned to him. "Do you like the room?"

He shrugged. "What's not to like? Plenty of toys to play with."

She nodded and followed his gaze to the shelves on either side of the bed. Body paints, flavored massage oils, oral sex gels and lotions – anything they could get in their mouths they could play with today.

Even food items like honey and chocolate syrup.

"Hungry?" he asked.

Her green eyes darkened. "For you."

She stood near the foot of the bed. He slid his arms around her waist and pulled her towards him. She smiled, threading her fingers through his hair.

"Any inhibitions about oral sex?" he asked, wanting to know what he could and couldn't do.

"Um, no. Although I don't have much experience in that area, either."

Michael sighed. So nearly untouched, and yet so fucking adventurous she took his breath away. Were all the men in Kansas complete morons?

"Have you ever sucked a cock, Serena?"

"Yes. Once or twice."

"Ever had a guy come in your mouth?"

"No."

His cock twitched, clamoring to be the first. "Had your pussy licked?"

"Sorta. Not to orgasm. They just did it as a quickie foreplay thing, you know?"

So, no man had brought her to orgasm by licking her pussy. This should be fun. And he had to admit, the idea of him giving her a "first" excited him. "Then we'll just have to figure out what you *do* like, won't we?"

She nodded and licked her lips.

Unable to wait any longer, Michael slid his hands over her shoulders and down her arms, feeling her slight shiver.

"Cold?"

"No. Excited."

He chuckled. She was so damn honest in her feelings. He'd make this a mind blowing experience for her.

He pressed a soft kiss against her lips, then pressed on, coaxing her mouth open so he could slide his tongue inside. She met his tongue with hers, eagerly twining and sucking until his raging hard-on knocked on his pants for attention.

Keeping his gaze focused on her, he slowly undid the laces of her shirt, pulled it apart and reached for her breasts. She stepped forward and thrust her distended nipples into his waiting hands.

"You have gorgeous nipples, Serena. I want my mouth on them. I want to suck them until you beg me to fuck you."

Her rapid heartbeat thrummed against his hands and her breathing quickened. He loved how easily she became aroused.

Slipping the shirt off her shoulders, he left her skirt on and sat her on the bed, kneeling before her. He scanned the shelves next to him and grabbed a bottle of chocolate body paint.

"You like chocolate?" she asked.

"I like your breasts," he replied. "But it might be fun to play a little."

He opened the bottle, inhaling the sweet aroma of cocoa beans, and carefully spread a splotch of the dark creamy substance across her neck, down over her collarbone and

Jaci Burton

around her breasts. When he spread the paint over each of her nipples, she sucked in a breath and moaned.

After capping the bottle, he pulled her knees apart and nestled between her legs, pulling her towards him. Her sweet fragrance mingled with the chocolate, and he gently licked the syrup off her neck, feeling her shiver against him.

Following the trail of body paint, he stroked his tongue down the length of her throat, over her collarbone, and down to one breast, taking his time, coaxing her response, building her anticipation.

Then he took one, slow swipe of her nipple with his tongue.

She hissed and arched her back, forcing the erect bud further inside his mouth. He sucked it in, swirling his tongue around the hard pebble, then moved to the other nipple and did the same. She wound her fingers through his hair and pushed his mouth against her breasts.

He could spend all day buried between her breasts, but there was much more of her he wanted to explore.

"Lie down on the bed," he commanded.

With a quick tug, he yanked her skirt off and parted her legs, ogling her shaved pussy. Damn, it was a beautiful sight. Wet, with her cream flowing down her lips to the crack of her ass.

"You're wet already, Serena. Are you ready for this?"

"Yes, Michael. Please," she begged, squirming.

"Let's try something different." He turned once again to the shelves, selecting a bottle of erotic butter.

"A little butter for your muffin," he said with a laugh.

She lifted her head and watched him pour the butter rum flavored lotion over the top of her pussy. It slid down over her clit, her lips, and into the crack of her ass.

She gasped. "It's cold."

"You'll be warm in a minute," he promised, then bent his head towards the pussy he'd been wanting to get his mouth on for days. He inhaled her sweet fragrance, but waited, watching her, knowing she anticipated his tongue, wanting her to suffer just a few seconds longer.

"Michael. Please."

"Please, what? Tell me what you want, Serena," he whispered.

"Lick me. Suck my clit. Make me come."

With a growl of pure animal lust he bent down and slowly swiped his tongue over her clit. She cried out and lifted her hips off the bed. Sliding his hands under her ass, he covered her slit with his mouth, sucking the distended nub between his lips.

The mixture of the flavored butter and her natural taste was heaven. He pressed his tongue flat against her clit, circling the distended nub over and over again until she writhed beneath him, her desire flowing over his chin.

"Oh, God, Michael, Oh God, I can't take this. Please, please."

He knew she was mindless with passion, didn't even know what she was saying. Her moans, her movements nearly drove him over the edge, but he focused on her, wanting this to be spectacular for her. He moved his mouth lower and slid his tongue deep inside her, stroking it in and out like he would if it were his cock. She gasped and grabbed his head, pulling him closer.

Then he replaced his tongue with his fingers, gently probing against her flesh until he slid one inside, then two. She bucked off the bed as he relentlessly stroked her pussy with his fingers, once again taking her clit between his lips and gently sucking and licking.

"I'm going to come," she rasped.

She wasn't kidding. She cried out and her pussy contracted tightly against his fingers. Her come poured out over his hand as she kept at it, moaning and lifting her hips, her hands clenching the sheets on the bed. He lapped her up greedily, her intoxicating flavor driving him crazy.

Moments later, she relaxed, still panting, her legs shaking with aftershocks.

Michael's cock felt like stone—aching, pulsing with the need to plunge inside Serena's sopping wet pussy and come like he'd never come before.

It took all the restraint he had not to jump up and drive deep inside her. Instead, he climbed up on the bed and pulled her against him while she recovered her breathing.

"Wow," she whispered against his chest.

He smiled. "Good?"

"Mmm hmm. Fantastic. I never knew an orgasm could feel that good. The ones I give myself are nice, but nothing like that."

He shook his head, thinking about all the years Serena had spent 'doing it herself.' Weren't there any men where she lived who recognized what a desirable woman lived among them?

Serena looked up at Michael and smiled, feeling more content than she had in some time. He'd just given her the best orgasm of her life, and now it was time to reciprocate.

She leveled a serious look at him. "Now it's my turn. I'm going to surround your cock with my lips and take you in as deep as I can. I'm going to suck it deep and make you come."

His eyes darkened, and he gave her a lethal smile. "Give it your best shot."

She sat up on the bed and pushed her hair out of her face. The remnants of chocolate body paint still clung to her breasts.

"Let's see," she said. "How about 'Giving Great Head Oral Lotion'? In cinnamon, I think, for a little tingle action."

"Whatever you want," he said, his voice husky. "Just get your mouth on my cock."

She shivered at his command, knowing how much he had to be aching for release.

She slipped off the bed and reached for the bottle, then turned to him. "Stand up, Michael."

He stood quickly and she grasped his shorts, pulling them down his hips until they pooled at his feet. When he started to sit on the bed, she stopped him.

Serena placed an oversized pillow on the floor, and then dropped to her knees before him.

He sucked in a breath and looked down at her. She felt wicked in this subservient position, feeling for all the world like his slave, and loving every minute of it.

"You want me to watch you suck my cock this way?" he said, his voice tight with need.

"That's exactly what I want."

After uncapping the bottle, she poured some of the flavored lotion onto her palms and spread it over both her hands. She grasped his engorged shaft, sliding the lotion all over. The heat of his cock and the cool lotion were a potent combination, and she felt her body thrum to life. His shaft jumped in her hands and he groaned.

She looked up at him, smiled and leaned forward, taking just the tip into her mouth.

The head of his cock was satiny soft, and she closed her lips over it and sucked him in, inch by inch. The cinnamon tingled in her mouth, and she could imagine the tingle stimulated his cock, too.

"You have a great mouth, Serena," he managed through gasps. "Suck it in deep. Yeah, like that."

His words encouraged her. She took him in all the way in until the head bobbed against the back of her throat, and then she took him deeper, as far as she could, until she couldn't take any more of his length.

"Fuck! That's good, baby."

He grabbed the back of her head and slowly fucked her mouth, in and out. The feel of his cock sliding back and forth through her lips got her juices flowing all over again.

His movements increased, but she wanted to prolong the pleasure for him. Not yet, she thought. Not quite yet.

She sat back, admiring the way his penis glistened with moisture, and stroked the length of him with both hands.

"I don't know what I like more. Your hands on me, or that sweet mouth."

"Do you like the way I suck your cock, Michael?"

"Oh yeah, baby. You like sucking it?"

"Yes. I like it a lot. It's hard and soft at the same time, and it jerks in my mouth when I suck it."

While she spoke she continued to stroke the length of him from shaft to tip, then took his balls in her hand and lightly tugged. She drew closer, stroking it while she bent down and lathed her tongue over his balls.

"Christ!" he groaned, tilting his head back and squeezing his eyes shut for a second. Then he looked down at her again. She felt the quiver of his legs against her each time she swiped her tongue over his tight balls.

Grasping his hips, she took him again in her mouth and began pumping her lips back and forth, her mouth gliding over the head.

"Yeah," he rasped. "Yeah, like that. I'm gonna come baby. Deep in that sweet mouth of yours."

He grasped her hair and held her there, his body trembling. She swiped her tongue around the sensitive head and he let loose a guttural moan. His balls drew up tight against her hand. With a forceful thrust of his hips he ejaculated into her mouth.

Serena swallowed every drop of his sweet juice, then licked slowly until she felt his body relax. He collapsed on the bed and she sat on her heels, smiling up at him.

"Christ, Serena," he said, shaking his head. "I've never had a blow job like that before."

Heat rose to her face. Surely a man as worldly as Michael had experienced plenty of great sex before. He was just being kind to her. But his compliment warmed her.

Climbing up on the bed, she snuggled next to him, resting her head against his shoulder. He wrapped his arms around her, and for a few minutes neither of them spoke. Serena was content just listening to his heartbeat.

She trailed her fingertip over his chest, wrapping her fingers around the curling hairs there. She sighed and scooted closer to him, already anticipating the next time.

"I need a bath," he murmured, pressing a kiss to the top of her head.

"Me too." Her chocolate covered breasts stuck to his chest.

Michael rose from the bed and turned on the tub, then came back a few minutes later and held out his hand for her. He pulled her up against him, and pressed a light kiss to her lips.

She tasted herself on his lips. Sinfully erotic, knowing they'd been so intimate, unlike anything she'd ever experienced before, or likely would again. At least, not after this week.

He stepped into the tub and held out his hand, helping her, then settled her in front of him, her back resting against his chest.

The warm water felt good. Lying in Michael's arms felt better.

These moments where they snuggled together, without thoughts of sex between them, were surprisingly the most intimate.

Okay, maybe they were still thinking of sex. At least she was. But right now, the game was on pause.

He picked up a sponge and ran it over her shoulders and across her breasts, erasing all traces of the sticky chocolate.

"Did you enjoy that?" he asked, whispering in her ear.

She shivered at the low rumble of his voice. "Yes. Very much." Half turning, she met his gaze. "You?"

"Hell yeah. You're fantastic. I can't believe you're so inexperienced."

She smiled.

"You must be a quick study," he teased, reaching around to tickle her ribs. She shrieked with laughter and threw water at him until he pulled her against his chest again.

She settled against him, completely content and supremely pleased with herself. For a novice at these things, so far, she seemed to be doing all right.

Chapter Seven

ஐ

"How often do you masturbate, Serena?"

Serena almost dropped her fork at Michael's question. Interesting dinner conversation, to say the least.

After their relaxing bath, they'd gone back to their room to change and Michael suggested they have dinner at the resort restaurant. She was all for that. It would almost be like a date.

"Why do you want to know?" she asked, laying her fork on the plate and taking a sip of wine. The soft jazz playing and the florally scented ocean breeze cast an ambiance about the place incongruent with the subject of their conversation. Then again, Serena had found nothing about this week so far had been 'typical.'

He shrugged, his white, even teeth gleaming in the semi darkness of the tropically decorated room. His dark tan accentuated the ocean blue of his eyes. "Just wondered. You don't seem to have much of an active sex life. And you said you masturbated frequently. I was just curious as to how often."

"Usually every day," she said, figuring there was no point in trying to hide anything from him. First off, he knew her more intimately than anyone ever had. Second, they wouldn't be continuing their relationship beyond this one week together, so what did it matter what she told him?

He arched a brow and took a drink. "Daily? Are you horny a lot?"

"I guess I must be." Recalling her boring, lonely existence in Kansas wasn't how she wanted to finish off this day.

Thinking about the oral delights they'd shared earlier — that was more to her liking.

"How do you do it?"

"Do what? Masturbate?"

"Yeah."

"The usual way, I guess."

"More specific."

"Like what?"

Their waitress arrived, cleared their plates and offered them coffee, which they both declined.

The subject of masturbation temporarily cast aside with the completion of dinner, Michael scooped up the half-empty wine bottle and they left the restaurant.

Would this be another night where he would retreat to his room, leaving her alone? Maybe if she asked him to join her, they could watch a movie or do something together until bedtime.

After that she'd climb into her bed alone, as usual, thinking about the man sleeping across the hall. She'd wondered what he'd do if she went to his room, crawled under the covers, and asked him to simply hold her all night long.

Ridiculous, she reminded herself. Her relationship with Michael wasn't romantic. He wasn't even here to participate in these adventures, had merely agreed to do so for her. Not that he wasn't getting anything out of them. He certainly seemed to enjoy the sexual experiences they'd shared together.

But sleeping with her? Holding her close all night? Now that was another matter, and one she vowed she wouldn't broach with him. No matter how much she longed to sleep in his arms.

When they entered their suite, Serena waited for Michael to say goodnight. Instead, he took the bottle of wine to the kitchen and opened it, returning to the living area with two glasses.

He surprised her. He wasn't going to his room. In fact, he sat on the sofa next to her. Close enough that his leg brushed against hers, igniting her seemingly never quenchable sexual fires.

"Do you touch yourself mostly at night?" he asked, resurrecting their earlier conversation.

Surprisingly, she didn't mind discussing such an intimate subject with him. In fact, she found it exciting. Like talking dirty with a man. "Usually. On the weekends it could be any time."

"Tell me how you do it. On the bed, or in another room?"

"Depends," she explained, circling the rim of the wine glass with her fingertip.

"On?"

She shifted her feet underneath her, her sundress falling in silk waves over her thighs. Michael watched her every movement. "On where I am, what I'm doing, when the mood hits me."

Arching a brow, he grinned. "Just drop wherever you are and go at it?"

Laughing, she shook her head. "Not quite like that."

He brushed her hair away from her face, the gesture so personal it almost brought tears to her eyes. She could almost believe he actually cared about her, if she allowed herself to think that way. Which she wouldn't. Bringing emotion into their relationship would only lead to hurt.

"Do you use movies? Fantasize? Magazines or books?"

She held out the glass while he poured more wine. "That depends, too. If it's at night, sometimes I'll pop in a movie."

"That's right. You said you have a video collection of porn."

"I don't know if it's a collection, but I have a few movies."

"You like videos?"

"Yes." She heard the breathlessness of her voice, knew he was getting to her again, making her want him. But they didn't have an 'event' tonight. And so far they'd managed to confine their sex play to their official adventures. Would tonight be different?

"Have you ever engaged in mutual masturbation with someone?"

After a quick swallow of wine, she shook her head. "No. Have you?"

"Yeah. It's pretty hot to watch someone get themselves off."

Her nipples rose and pressed against the soft silk of her dress. Thinking about a scene like that was more than she could hope for. The thought of doing it right here with Michael pooled instant moisture between her legs.

He was such a sexual adventurer. Just the kind of man she wished she could find in her town. But how? Other than the occasional dates and the few disastrous relationships she'd had, there'd been no one. She'd finally given up, figuring she was wasting her time and the man's if he wasn't going to be able to push her erotic buttons.

Maybe a man like Michael *was* out there somewhere. But it didn't figure she'd find him in her backyard.

His eyes darkened and he took the glass from her hand and set it on the table, along with his. "Would you like to do that, Serena?"

"You mean someday?" she asked, knowing that wasn't his question.

"No. I mean tonight. Right now. With me."

Blood roared in her ears and her body fired up hot and ready. "I…I don't know."

"Scary?"

Was it? Or was it because masturbation seemed so personal, so private? She'd never touched herself in front of anyone before. Nor had she ever seen anyone masturbate, other than in the movies she owned.

"Not scary. Just new."

He swirled a finger over the swell of her breasts revealed in the gap of her sundress. Sliding a thumb over her already hardened nipple, he smiled when she let out a gasp.

"I think you want this. I think it excites the hell out of you."

He was right, dammit. It did, and she did. She wanted this. Wanted to watch what a man did when he took his cock in his hand, wanted his eyes on her when she brought herself to orgasm.

Besides, if they did, it would fall outside the realm of their scheduled events, and that was intriguing enough.

"Yes," she admitted, all but breathless with anticipation. "I want this."

"Would you like me to put a movie in the player? Something we could watch to give us a little visual turn on, until we watch each other?"

"Yes." Although she doubted she'd be able to take her eyes off Michael.

He quickly selected a movie, then arranged the two single chairs in the room so they'd face each other, and still be able to see the television.

"How do we go about this?" she asked, not sure what to do and not wanting to appear more naïve than she already had.

"Just relax," he said, getting comfortable in the chair. "Watch the movie, then do what comes naturally. When you want to watch what I'm doing, then watch."

Serena couldn't believe she was actually going to touch herself in front of Michael. She wasn't even sure she'd be able to make herself come with him watching. It wasn't the same as doing it in the privacy of her own house. Then again, she never thought she'd be able to do half the things she'd done so far this week, and with a complete stranger. Yet she had.

Maybe it was because Michael had never seemed like a stranger to her.

The movie began, one of the new releases she'd heard about. This one had one man, two women. They undressed him, stroked him, took turns taking his cock into their mouths. The man in the movie had a tremendously long cock. Both women stroked him with their hands. Serena couldn't help but get turned on at the visual, watching the close-ups of the two women sucking the man. Deep veins ridged along the sides of his shaft. When the two women's lips touched while running their mouths along his penis she groaned in pleasure.

Her hand found its way to her breasts, kneading and stroking the aching mounds before circling her nipples with the tips of her fingers. She pulled the top of her dress down and gathered her breasts in her hands, alternatively flicking and pinching her nipples.

The women in the video then turned to each other while the man watched and stroked his own cock. They undressed each other, sucking nipples and trailing hands over asses and pussies. The blonde dipped her finger into the other woman's pussy, pulling it out and licking the juices off. Then the dark haired girl dropped to her knees and fit her mouth over the blonde's mound and sucked her clit.

Serena shuddered at the erotic play between the two women. She swept her hand over her belly and moved downward.

Michael's heavy breathing reminded her she wasn't alone. He still wore his shorts and tank top, but his hand rested on his crotch and he rubbed his shaft through the material. Watching him touch himself like that was an erotic turn on like nothing Serena had ever expected.

His hard cock pressed against his shorts. Without taking his eyes off her, he lifted his hips and pulled his shorts down around his knees, taking his cock in his hands, stroking it slowly. Serena focused on the dark hairs at the base of his shaft, the purple head of his engorged cock, the way he wrapped his fingers around it, so different than the way she touched him.

His movements mesmerized her. She felt like she was in the classroom, experiencing a monumental revelation.

How To Stroke A Cock 101, she thought to herself, her lips curving into a smile.

She could teach him a few things, too. Slowly, deliberately, she lifted the hem of her dress, revealing her pussy to him.

"You're wet," he said, focusing his heated gaze between her legs. As soon as he'd looked at her pussy the grip on his shaft tightened and his strokes became longer.

"Yes." And getting wetter by the second.

The sight of him stroking his shaft heated her blood to boiling. So amazingly erotic, watching him, knowing he watched her. Any hesitation she might have felt at touching herself in front of him disappeared. She was completely into pleasuring herself, and pleasuring him with her actions.

In fact, she could come right now if she touched that certain spot, moved her fingers a certain way. But she didn't want to. She wanted to hold off, watch Michael, see how he stroked himself, how much enjoyment he generated from doing what she did.

They focused only on each other, the movie no more than panting, grunting background noise. Sex permeated the air around her, both the scent of her and him mingling as a powerful aphrodisiac.

"You like this?" he asked. He took his thumb and circled the ridge under the head of his cock, squeezing hard, much harder than she would have ever touched him.

"Yes," she said, gasping as she increased the tempo of her strokes to match his.

He looked pained, almost, his face scrunched into a concentrated frown as his strokes quickened even more. He breathed through his mouth, like her, raised his hips in time to his strokes, like her.

Serena tweaked her nipples with one hand, the other busily strumming her clit. When she slid two fingers into her snatch, she thought Michael was going to leap out of the chair. He groaned.

"Taste them," he commanded. "Suck your juices off your fingers."

Slipping her fingers out of her soaked pussy, she slowly raised them to her lips and wrapped her mouth around them, sucking them in as if she were sucking his cock.

"Christ!" he shouted, his gaze riveted on her. "That's so fucking hot."

Shivers racked her body at his words. Knowing she pleased him increased her own pleasure ten fold. "I'm going to come soon," she rasped, knowing she couldn't hold out much longer. Between his encouragement and watching him furiously stroke his shaft, she couldn't hold back.

"Yeah," he said. "Come on baby, show me how you do it. Make yourself come for me."

She felt the first tingling waves of her orgasm and adjusted her fingers to hit that sensitive spot on her clit that would drive her over. Keeping her eyes focused on Michael, she let out a low moan that grew into a howl of pleasure with her rising orgasm.

Michael shifted back and let loose a stream of come that shot clear across the room. She'd never seen a man make himself come, and vowed this wouldn't be the only time it happened.

Instead of dwindling in intensity, it increased. The waves of her orgasm still pulsed against her questing fingers, creamy come pouring between the cheeks of her ass, soaking the chair. She panted in an effort to suck in oxygen, trying to slow down the pummeling heartbeats that pounded her body.

Eventually, they both slowed their movements and watched each other breathe. Ropes of come lined the floor between them, and Serena smiled in satisfaction as if she'd personally stroked that streaming jet of jism out of him.

Still, neither of them seemed in a hurry to move. Michael continued to slowly massage his shaft while Serena trailed her fingers lightly over her now sensitive lips.

He smiled at her. "Did you enjoy that?"

She nodded and returned the smile, not the least bit embarrassed. "I enjoyed it very much. Do you think we could do it again sometime?"

His eyes darkened like storm clouds. "Definitely. You're incredible, Serena."

"You're not too bad yourself," she replied. Which was a lie. He was fantastic. Everything she'd ever wanted in a lover. And at that, they hadn't even fucked yet.

"I'm going to fuck you good tomorrow," he said, his voice husky with promise.

"Yes, I know."

Tomorrow couldn't come soon enough for her. Tomorrow was the day she'd finally feel that big cock stuffed inside her, stretching her, hitting that sensitive G-spot inside her until she came in roaring waves all over his shaft.

If these past few days had been an indicator of what it would be like to fuck Michael, she wasn't sure she'd survive the pleasure.

But she'd certainly be willing to die trying.

They both adjusted their clothes. Serena was aware of the silence between them. Though not uncomfortable, she always wondered what he was thinking when he went silent like that.

He was such an amazing man. So full of life and adventure, so smart, so creative, and so willing to accommodate her.

She felt the stirrings in her heart when she looked at him, the warning signals blasting at her from all directions.

No. She couldn't let it happen, couldn't allow herself to feel anything for him other than physical pleasure.

But as he smiled at her, she knew it was already too late.

* * * * *

Michael cursed inwardly. What the fuck had he just done?

Oh sure, he was all about keeping things between them impersonal, making sure their sex stayed within the parameters of the scheduled adventures.

So, what was the first thing he did? Suggested a little mutual masturbation in the living room. Was it a scheduled event? Not even fucking close.

How much more personal could that get?

And the worst thing was, he'd enjoyed the hell out of it. More than enjoyed it — it had damn near killed him. Never had he gotten off so hard and so fast. Serena was the hottest woman he'd ever met. Whatever he suggested, she was game for.

He hadn't thought a woman like her existed. Unfortunately, he'd been wrong.

She was so perfect for him it was scary. Beautiful, intelligent, sexy and erotic as hell.

Shit. He was fucked. Fucked, fucked, fucked. In the matter of a few short days, he'd let her wriggle under his radar and blindside him with a shot the size of a two thousand pound bomb.

"Would you like to sit on the couch with me? Watch some television or work on your book?"

She looked at him with such a hopeful expression, everything vulnerable about her so clearly written on her face, he felt like packing and heading home right that moment.

But he wouldn't. He might be an asshole, but even he wasn't that big an asshole.

"Sure. I've got a little work left to do anyway. Maybe you could help me with it."

Ah, hell. Her face brightened, tingeing pink along her tanned cheeks, and she smiled so wide one would think he'd just gifted her with the Hope Diamond. And all he'd done was agree to sit next to her.

Damn, she was easy to live with. And damn if he didn't feel the stirrings of emotion across his scarred old heart.

This wasn't his fault. He'd come to Paradise Resort to relax and research, maybe get in a little hot sex with Ginny. No entanglements, pleasure and work combined— it was supposed to be perfect.

Instead, this plain little blonde had showed up on his doorstep in need of a little help. No big deal, right? Yeah, right. Then she'd turned into Wonder Sex Woman while he wasn't looking and proceeded to twist his balls in a knot until he walked behind her drooling.

And if that wasn't bad enough, she batted those innocent green eyes at him and made him *feel*. He didn't want to feel. He didn't want to enjoy being around her. He didn't want to think about how much he enjoyed both fucking her and talking to her.

This week *would* end. They'd go their separate ways, and whatever fun they'd had together would be over.

He knew it, but it sure as hell seemed like she didn't. He mentally cursed at the nagging feeling of guilt worming its way inside him.

Well, fuck it. She was a big girl, she knew what she was getting into. He'd warned her there could be no emotional involvement, and she'd agreed. So if she got hurt, that was her problem, not his.

And if he got hurt? Then that's what he'd deserve for allowing feelings to get in the way of fucking.

Chapter Eight

෩

"Your female character had to have something horrible happen in her past to make her act in such an evil way," Serena pointed out, smiling at Michael's frown.

"Why? Couldn't she just have been born that way?"

"Hardly. No one kills without reason. Even insanity has a cause. Familial, psychological trauma—"

He waved his hand at her. "Bullshit. She's always been a vicious bitch from hell, and nothing's going to change that."

Serena sat cross-legged on the sofa, Michael's notes spread out on her lap. They'd been at this ever since last night, when they'd talked for hours until neither could stay awake. Then they'd gotten on it right after breakfast again, brainstorming and throwing out ideas for his new book.

She loved that he'd asked for her opinion. After having read all his books, she considered herself somewhat of an expert on his characters. Funny how he wasn't taking all that well to her suggestions, though.

But instead of irritating her, his disgruntled reaction both amused and invigorated her. For all intents and purposes, Michael wrote erotica. He could call it erotic criminal fiction, but it was erotica.

Right up her literary alley.

"Michael, look," she said, pulling off her glasses and placing them gently on top of the pile of papers. "This woman, Victoria as you've named her, wasn't brought up to kill and dismember men. Something had to serve as a catalyst to make her kill the first time. One doesn't go through life perfectly happy for twenty-five years, then one day wake up and decide

89

to go on a serial killing spree and lop off every man's penis who gets in her way."

"I realize that," he said, his face buried in the laptop. "What I'm saying is you want her to have experienced a psychological trauma, when all it would really take is a loose screw in her head to pop."

Serena smiled. "Yes, it's true that could happen. The point I'm trying to get across is that your readers will be more enticed if you lay a little background on her — make something happen to her in the past that gives her the impetus to kill."

He glanced up, his gaze meeting hers. God his eyes were blue. She lost herself in them every time he looked at her.

"You might have a point," he said, still considering her.

She warmed under his gaze, feeling as if she'd actually been helpful. "I've done quite a bit of research into psychoses and triggers for violent crimes."

"Why?"

With a shrug, she said, "Nothing better to do on a Saturday night. Besides, one of the psychology professors at the college had asked for my help."

He quirked a brow. "Someone you dated?"

Did she sense a little male jealousy in that question? No, just her imagination. "Hardly. I never date other faculty members."

"Why not?"

"I already told you. I couldn't...do what I do with you with any of them."

"Again, why not?"

She sighed. "Not conducive to tenure to get caught fucking one of the other professors. Besides, what if I started dating one of my colleagues, and it led to sex? Then what am I supposed to do, suggest we engage in a little mutual masturbation or voyeurism? Come on, Michael, be realistic.

My tastes sexually run to the, uh, unusual. I'm not a plain vanilla kind of woman."

"Thank God," he said, those intense blue eyes penetrating her defenses.

One of the things she loved most about him was his appreciation for her sexual appetite. He didn't find her desires bizarre at all. "There you have it. I couldn't enjoy a boring sexual routine with a man, and I certainly won't reveal my true nature to anyone where I live."

He graced her with a boyish grin. "So, you're kinda stuck between a rock and no hard place, then."

She giggled at his pun. "You could say that."

Michael put the laptop on the table and approached her, lifting the paperwork off her lap.

She pulled down the nightshirt where it had ridden up her thighs, her body heating when Michael yanked it back up her legs again. He settled in next to her and took her hands in his.

"Serena, how will you ever be happy?"

What kind of question was that? She didn't want to think about happiness. "I am happy."

"Are you?"

"Yes." She wasn't lying. Right now, with him, she was as happy as she'd ever been.

"What about when you go back to Kansas? What then?"

"Then my life resumes, same as it was before I came here."

"And that'll be enough for you?"

Did she have a choice? "It'll have to be."

"That doesn't make sense," he said, leaning back and running his fingers through his hair.

She sensed his frustration, but didn't understand it. Why would he even care how she lived her life, or what happened to her after she left the resort? They weren't involved and never would be.

"What doesn't make sense? That I choose to live my life a certain way, and that you might not agree with it?"

"I think you're hiding. I think you refuse to make the necessary changes in your life so you'll be happy."

She crossed her arms, not liking at all the way the conversation had turned. Why couldn't he just let things be? "Leave it alone, Michael. I've lived this way for years, and it works for me."

He stood and paced the room. "It works for you. No dating, no relationship, no romance. The only sex you get is what you do yourself. That is, until you save up enough money to come to a place like this and let a stranger fuck your brains out for a week. Is that really what you want? Is that the map for the rest of your life?"

Serena stood too, furious at Michael for putting in to words what she'd so expertly denied for so many years. She advanced on him, stopping when they were nose to nose.

"How dare you presume to know anything about my life, or what makes me happy? You don't know a damn thing about me, so just back off!"

"Coward. You just don't wanna face the fact that your life is miserable. And all this time I gave you credit for being smart."

"Are you insinuating otherwise?" she asked, lowering her voice so she wouldn't squeal like she really wanted to.

"You figure it out. For someone who seems to know exactly what she wants from sex, you sure suck at figuring out the rest of your life."

No more. She refused to listen to any more of his rantings. "I don't need to stand here and take this."

"No, I guess you don't."

The air was charged with the tension between them. It enveloped her, sucked her in and made her feel weak.

No. She wasn't weak. She'd never been weak. She knew exactly what she was doing. Her life was her choice. Screw Michael Donovan for making her feel as if she was going about it all wrong.

Without another word she stormed from the room and slammed the door to her bedroom. Mumbling under her breath the entire time she yanked on shorts and a tank top, grabbed her sandals and beach bag and threw open the door.

"Where are you going?" he asked, anger still evident in his tone.

She didn't even make eye contact with him as she walked past. "To the beach. For a walk. I don't know. Out."

She threw open the door to the suite, banging it against the wall in a loud crash. Despite feeling guilty at manhandling the door, she slammed it shut behind her.

If she was lucky, she'd be able to close the door on the doubts Michael had opened.

* * * * *

Michael cursed as he stepped outside on the balcony, the ever cooling breeze chilling him.

Fuck. The weather had changed. He could tell by the ominous dark clouds over the ocean that a storm was coming. And Serena was still out there, somewhere.

He'd already checked the beach, the cabanas and the restaurant. No sign of her, and no one recalled seeing her.

She'd left over three hours ago. Where could she be?

He'd even contacted Morgan to see if she'd signed in unscheduled on one of the adventures. She hadn't. He'd been relieved to know that she wasn't experiencing some erotic pleasures without him. And then had proceeded to cuss himself out for nearly fifteen minutes for even caring who she fucked.

But now that a storm loomed near the island, he wanted her back. In the room. Safe.

With him.

And if she wasn't coming back, then he'd damn well go out there to find her, then drag her back by the hair if he had to.

The light drizzle had already started, the wind picking up the droplets and hurtling them sideways onto the balcony.

Michael closed the sliding glass door, grabbed his tennis shoes and ran out the door.

Damn woman. Didn't know enough to come in out of the rain.

By the time he stepped outside the rain had increased. Fat globs of water pelted him as he ran through the garden path. No one was about.

Oh sure. All the sensible people had taken shelter inside.

Not him. He was out here looking for a lunatic. And God help her when he found her.

He slipped his jacket on, thankful he'd thought to grab it as he ran out the door. The temperature hadn't dropped that much, but after all the days of tropical warmth the breeze and rain seemed cold.

Plus, it was really fucking windy. Morgan had cautioned him against going outside, saying the weather report indicated severe weather for the next several hours.

Shit. Just great. He wasn't being insensible. Serena was. And now he had to be out in the pouring rain to search for her.

But where? The island wasn't huge, by any means, but it certainly wasn't tiny, either. Besides the resort area, there were roughly two hundred square miles of island to explore. Not that she'd have gotten that far, but if he had to search the entire island to find her they were both gonna be in deep shit.

By the time he'd checked in every building the resort had, he knew she wasn't anywhere close. Which meant he'd have to follow the walking trail past the resort and into the jungle-like rain forest.

In the rain.

The driving, windy rain.

Shit.

He should just turn around and head back to his room and let her fend for herself. She was the one who'd left in a huff. Let her figure out how to survive in the rain.

If he were as big a prick as he thought himself, he'd do that.

But he wasn't. So he trekked on, past the resort property and onto the walking trail.

At least he had some relief from the rain here. The tall, dense tropical trees and foliage protected him somewhat from the downpour. But the trail floor was quickly filling with water, evidenced by his squishing tennis shoes.

He'd walked for almost an hour, the steady downpour pummeling him. He shivered from the soaking he'd gotten and was determined to turn around and call out the experts for help.

Then he spotted it. A little palm frond covered building. Sort of like a beach shack, only a little bigger, with a thatched, sloping roof.

Sitting calmly on the front porch watching it rain, was Serena.

She spotted him, smiled and waved.

Just like that. As if being this far away from the resort was no big deal.

Could he kill her, he wondered? He knew all the ways to do it. He'd done it in his books hundreds of times. Quick, painless — no, he took that back. He'd like her to suffer.

Claro

"What are you doing here?" she asked, quickly pulling a towel from the stack behind her and offering it to him.

He yanked the towel from her hands. "I was looking for you," he growled, his temper not getting any better just because he'd found her.

She frowned, seemingly confused as to why he would have been searching for her. "Why?"

"Because you've been gone four hours."

She shrugged. "I took a walk. The trail looked interesting so I thought I'd explore. Then it started to rain, so when I found this place I figured I'd better stop here and wait it out."

The more nonchalant she played this out, the more annoyed Michael became. "Do you know I looked everywhere for you? I checked every building and with every staff member at the resort. No one claimed to have seen you. I had no fucking idea where you were!" He threw the wet towels on the floor of the shack and fixed a vicious glare on her.

Her lips curved in a smile. A smile!

"You were worried about me?"

"No."

"Yes, you were. It's very sweet."

"It is not sweet. I am not sweet. Dammit, I'm pissed as hell. I'm half drowned here, there's a potential hurricane on the way, and you're sitting there smiling at me like it's no fucking big deal!"

She stepped toward him with another towel in hand, her green eyes glistening. Were those tears in her eyes?

"You're still dripping," she said, reaching around him to fluff his hair.

He grabbed her wrists. "I don't need you to coddle me. I'm fine."

"You came out in the rain to look for me," she whispered, eyes welling with more moisture.

Shit. No crying. Crying was a female ploy to make men forget they were madder than a bull in a coliseum filled with matadors. He grabbed her arms and pinned them to her sides. "No big deal."

"It is to me."

The storm picked up again, lashing the palm fronds around the shack with wind and streams of rain.

Inside the shack a storm brewed of near equal intensity. Michael could feel it raging between them.

He had a tenuous hold on the remnants of his sanity. If she took one step towards him, he wouldn't be responsible for what happened.

She took one step towards him, and all was lost.

He swept her into his arms and took her saucy mouth in a ravaging kiss.

Chapter Nine

ನಿ

Serena gasped as Michael fit his mouth none too gently to hers, felt his raging need equaling her own.

The argument they'd just had was only a prelude, a dance of sorts, around a sensual fire that blazed hotter than anything she could comprehend. An incredible need for him began to build, a need she'd felt from the first moment she'd laid eyes on him.

A need which had grown in intensity over the past several days.

She was on fire for him, and wanted, needed him to burn deep inside her. She craved that joining with him, knew if she didn't have it she'd wither up and die.

His mouth brushed hot against her lips, coaxing her to open up for him. She did, and he swept his tongue inside, melting her. Moisture pooled between her legs, so familiar, so welcome.

He pushed her damp hair to the side and slid his tongue over her neck and throat, kissing and nibbling, finally sinking his teeth into that tender spot on her shoulder. She shivered and moaned, the pain and pleasure mingling until near unbearable.

Words weren't necessary and she couldn't have found any to say. She wanted only to feel right now — his hands and mouth on her skin quenching that fire he raised over her flesh. Words, she was afraid, would break the spell — bring about a reality that she simply could not, would not face right now.

Reality would come later. Now was for desire, for passion, for unbridled lust, for pure enjoyment of everything physical with a man she'd come to care deeply about.

If that little niggling truth hit her right smack in her heart, she pushed it away for now. She'd worry about her feelings for Michael later. Now she simply wanted him, had to have him. Inside her, part of her, like she'd been craving her whole life.

She'd waited forever for him, and she was going to have him.

"I want those clothes off now," he commanded, stepping back from her. His eyes blazed as dark as the storm clouds covering the blue sky, and she shivered.

"Now, Serena."

His words thrilled her, knowing what would follow. This was no scripted event, no scheduled adventure. It was simply the two of them, a couple about to make love, to share the most intense experience two people could have together.

She fumbled with the buttons on her shorts, undoing them with shaky fingers until she managed to slide them down and step out of them, kicking them to the side. She pulled the tank top over her head and discarded it on a nearby shelf.

She stood in front of him wearing only her white silk thong panties, nothing more than a scrap of thin material covering her damp pussy. She felt the quivering deep inside, aching to feel his cock there, knowing how good it would feel once he plunged his huge shaft as far in as it would go.

His gaze flamed her senses as he assessed her from head to toe. She felt a blush heating her, surprised that she would feel even remotely shy when Michael looked at her. But then again, they'd never been as intimate as they were about to get. Yes, they'd shared sexual games. But that had been play. This was real.

At least for her.

He tore off his jacket and shirt, revealing the well-toned chest she loved to touch. He yanked his shorts down and kicked them away, then slipped out of his soaked tennis shoes.

His cock sprung from the thatch of dark hair between his legs, hard and pulsating with a life all its own. She longed to drop and take his shaft into her mouth and suck him hard until he came gallons all over her, but she forced herself to be patient.

There was a tiny room off the main shack. Michael pulled her in there and grabbed a sheet and some blankets to spread over the small bed.

This shack must have been used for sexual getaways. Completely isolated, it contained nothing but towels, blankets and the little bed. Maybe a place for staff members to steal away for a quickie? She didn't know, and frankly couldn't care less.

All she knew was the place had a bed, and she and Michael were going to use it. For that matter they could do it standing up or on the damp, wood-planked floor. She wanted his cock inside her and it was going to happen no matter the location.

Once again he pulled her towards him, this time laying her down on the mattress and sliding in next to her. The room was warm and dry, away from the pounding rain and wind outside.

His skin, though damp, burned as if he had a fever. She felt the fire singe her skin as he pulled her close, his hands closing over one aching breast.

She hissed out a breath when his thumb found her nipple, and moaned out loud when he lightly grazed it.

"You have very sensitive nipples," he murmured, leaning in to capture the tip in his mouth.

With a gasp she tilted her head back. Michael tugged her nipple between his teeth, the pleasure and pain excruciatingly erotic.

Her hands wound into his wet hair and she pulled his head to her breast, wanting him to take all of it into his hot, wet mouth. His other hand busily worked the other nipple, his rough hand sending sparks of pleasure to her pussy.

Juices dampened her panties further and she instinctively spread her legs, signaling her need to be fucked.

"You know I'm going to fuck you 'til you scream," he warned, taking her mouth again in fierce kisses that left her breathless.

"Yes," she managed between gasps. His hand trailed over her belly and lower.

"Tell me you want it, Serena."

Tell him? Tell him what? How could she tell him what she wanted when she couldn't form a coherent sentence to save her life? Desire and expectation fogged her thinking process. Couldn't he just touch her, kiss her, make love to her?

Why doesn't he know what I need? Because even she didn't know, that's why. She fought for the words that would convey the physical. He didn't want to know about the emotional. What she really wanted, what she craved desperately, he'd never be able to give her.

"I want you to fuck me. Hard, deep, ram that huge cock so far inside me your balls slap my ass."

He emitted a fierce growl and slipped his fingers inside her panties, finding and teasing her clit until she cried out.

"You're so hot. You make me want to fuck you hard and deep."

"Yes, Michael, hard. I need it hard and fast."

He bit lightly on her neck followed by a long lick of his tongue. "Yeah, baby. I'm going to give you one hard cock. Over and over and over again until you beg me to stop."

"Never," she said. "I'll never beg you to stop. I want you to fuck me so hard it hurts."

She'd never felt this way before. Never knew she could feel this way. It was almost like an out of body experience.

Someone else was feeling these sensations, uttering these words. Not her.

Michael threw one leg over hers and pulled her closer, his stiff cock riding against her hip. She reached for it, encircled it with her palm, and stroked the length of his shaft, rewarded with his groan of pleasure.

"Suck me," he demanded, rolling over onto his back and pulling her upright.

She straddled him, achingly aware of his cock jutting up against her pussy. He lifted his hips once, then twice, the head of his shaft sliding over her sensitive clit. She moaned, delighting in the sensation.

She bent down and grabbed his face between her hands. With all the passion she felt she kissed him, roughly as he'd done to her. His arms wound around her back, exploring her skin, his fingers sliding down the crevice of her backside, lightly touching her ass.

She ground her pussy against him and he groaned, "Fuck!" His passion thrilled her, spurred her on to new heights, made her want to please him like he'd never been pleased before.

Her movements slow and measured she moved down his body, stopping at his nipples to kiss and lick and stroke them until they'd hardened like hers. His belly quivered when she licked a trail from there to where the hair softened above his pubic bone.

His cock pulsated hot against her breasts and she gathered the globes together, capturing his shaft between them and stroking them up and down over his erection.

"Oh yeah, baby," he murmured, reaching for her hair and tugging at it lightly. "I'm going to fuck those, too."

She knew he was beyond reason, the same as she, and yet she delighted in this passion they shared. She planted kisses on his hips before moving her mouth over to the center, until finally her lips hovered over his quivering shaft.

Then she looked at him, and waited.

"Suck it," he rasped.

She complied, sliding her tongue over the sensitive head, licking the pre-come that had gathered at the tip, before closing her mouth over his swollen shaft and sliding it deeply into her mouth.

"Christ!" he groaned, grasping her head and pushing it down over his steel hard cock.

Serena sucked and rolled her tongue over the ridges in his shaft, exploring every taste, every texture. Slowly she took him all in, felt the heat bump the back of her throat. Relaxing and breathing deep, she swallowed him.

"Fuck, I can't take any more of this," he said, pulling her up and covering her lips with his, his tongue fucking her mouth with rhythmic strokes.

She panted like an animal. Which was exactly how she felt. The heady scent of sex and sweat mixed with the tropical smell of warm rain, a potent aphrodisiac.

Not that she needed any other stimulation. Michael's mouth and hands were more than enough.

Her hands reached for him, needing the contact of his skin against hers, but he pulled her hands away and flipped her over onto her back.

"I'm going to take you like this," he said, his eyes like hard sapphires.

Yes. This is the way she wanted him. On top of her, taking her, driving deep within her. She wanted him to dominate her, making her his completely.

He straddled her thighs, careful not to put any of his weight on her, and grasped her breasts with his hands, pulling at her nipples until she writhed and whimpered beneath him.

He circled her wrists, drawing her arms above her head. He used the fingertips of his free hand to blaze a heated trail between her breasts, over her belly, sliding his fingers over her hip.

Then he grasped her panties, fisted his hand around them and in one fierce tug ripped them away.

She gasped at the brutal pleasure of the act. Bared to the air and his gaze, her pussy throbbed near uncontrollably, spasms racking her body and juices flowing down her ass.

He stayed that way for a few seconds, his gaze focused on her pussy. One hand still held her wrists captive above her head. She couldn't have broken free if she tried.

She didn't want to.

She was his prisoner, his to do with whatever he wished.

"Tell me you want me, Serena. Just like this. No games, no schedule."

Her heart pounded against her ribcage at his serious tone. He wanted her, but not as part of the week's activities. This wasn't a preplanned function— he didn't want it be any more than she did.

"Make love to me, Michael," she said with what little breath remained in her lungs. "Make me yours."

With a fierce growl he spread her legs with his knee, keeping his gaze focused to hers.

The tip of his cock brushed her pussy lips and she could have cried out from the sheer pleasure of it.

A look of fierce concentration crossed his face. Serena wanted to brush that unruly lock of dark hair away from his forehead and draw his lips to hers for a kiss, but she couldn't—his hands still held her wrists imprisoned. It was both frustrating and erotic.

"We're gonna take this slow," he said, panting. "I want to feel every inch of that pussy on my cock when I slide inside you."

She felt the tremors already, knew she wouldn't be able to hold back for long. His slow, measured words were as tantalizing as the deliberate torture of his patient entry.

Inch by delicious inch she felt him enter her, his huge cock spreading her wide open, forcing an accommodation she wasn't accustomed to. And yet she took him in, easily, her pussy clamping down onto him and pulling him inside.

Deeper and deeper he pushed until he was fully sheathed within her. She breathed out a ragged sigh as he stilled, the corded muscles of his biceps straining to hold him above her.

"Damn that feels good," he murmured, his eyes closed and his breathing rapid and labored. With measured strokes he began to move within her.

She felt the contractions immediately, strong pulses of pleasure that assaulted her senses before she'd even had a chance to wrap her legs around his back.

"Oh, God, Michael, I'm coming!" she cried. He drew back and plunged hard within her. She heard the shrieks she knew were her own, but could do nothing to stop them as wave after wave of excruciating pleasure stabbed within her.

He held still while her orgasm poured through her, allowing her to feel his cock filling her. Her pussy continued to quake around his shaft until the tremors subsided.

Then he moved within her again, taking her up once again on a rack of delight. She couldn't believe the near constant state of arousal his cock provided. Despite her orgasm mere seconds ago, she felt it build within her once again.

"I love the feel of your pussy tightening around my cock," he whispered, relentless in his continued assault on her. Slowly at first, then increasing his thrusts until his balls slapped against her ass, his cock slamming hard within her.

He let go of her wrists and lay fully on top of her. She welcomed his hard chest crushing her breasts and wrapped her legs around his waist.

Her hands threaded through the soft thickness of his hair. She pulled his head down to hers. She ached to feel his lips on hers—needed the softness of his mouth as much as she needed his hard shaft penetrating her.

"You're so tight," he said, pulling out slowly so that only the head remained, brushing against that spot inside her pussy that drove her crazy. "Can you feel your pussy grab onto my cock and pull it back inside?"

She nodded, feeling the exquisite sensations he spoke about, knowing she was squeezing him, pulling at him, clamping around him.

"Fuck, I'm gonna come," he groaned and stepped up his thrusts, so hard he moved her across the bed. He raised up on his arms, his face contorted and let loose a yell as he pumped inside her.

Serena felt the pulses of his ejaculation and squeezed her legs around him, lifting her hips to get closer to his driving thrusts. At the same time it hit her again, a crashing wave of near unbearable pleasure that had her squeezing her legs around him and bucking up to meet his continued strokes.

Michael collapsed on top of her, their sweat soaked bodies joined, their breathing hard and labored.

She caressed his shoulders, feeling the tension ebb in the muscles, his breathing return to normal.

He withdrew but lay next to her, pulling her into his arms.

Nestled against his shoulder, Serena felt a contentment she'd never experienced.

Without a word he held her, stroked her hair and pulled her close. Finally, she felt his body relax and knew he'd fallen asleep.

She thought about this wondrous experience, and what it meant.

Knowing she shouldn't try to analyze it, but unable to help herself, she recounted the events of the past several days, marveling at the almost time-travel expediency of their relationship.

From strangers to playmates to lovers. She'd learned more about Michael in four days than she'd known about men she'd dated for months.

His kindness, his temper when he was riled, his sense of humor. No matter how he acted, she loved everything about him.

Her hand stilled on his back as the realization hit her.

She loved him. All of him. His wit, his humor, his handsome face and rugged body, his masculinity and the incredible way he made love to her. God help her, she'd done what she swore she wouldn't do.

She'd fallen in love with Michael.

Chapter Ten

ℬ

Michael woke with a start, not certain where he was. He kept his eyes closed, fatigue making him want to drift off again to wherever he'd been.

A warm body shifted against him, and he opened his eyes slowly, remembering.

Serena. He closed his eyes for a second and breathed in her fragrance. Ginger, mixed with rain. Fresh, sweet rain. Her hair was still damp, and softened by nature's bath. He ran his fingers through the tendrils and swept them away from her face.

He glanced down at the sleeping beauty he held in his arms. Her long lashes rested against her cheeks, full lips slightly parted, her cheeks and chin red from his beard.

His cock stirred to life. Not surprising. He wanted her again. And most likely again after that. If 'again' would always be like what they'd just experienced, he'd never tire of her.

She moaned in her sleep and snuggled closer against him. He wrapped his arms more fully around her, his instinct to protect and hold her outweighing any reservations he might have.

Like the fact he'd never had sex like that before.

He was no virgin, that was certain. And yet with her, the first time had been, well, the first time. Special, monumental even.

Shit. He ran his hand through his hair and blew out a breath. This couldn't be happening. He wouldn't let it happen. No emotion, remember?

And yet what they'd just had together was the most emotional experience he could remember since...

Since Mari. The woman he'd loved. The one he'd given his heart to, and married. The one who'd stomped on it and handed it back to him crumpled and bleeding.

Not again. Never again.

Despite the incredible sexual experience, what they'd just done was a one time thing. His emotions were getting involved, and he'd just have to —

"How long have you been awake?"

He looked down at sleepy green eyes and a soft smile. She reached up and traced the stubble of beard along his jaw line, then swept her finger over his lips, leaned up and kissed him.

Well, hell. Maybe one more time. But that was all. Then it was over.

"Not long," he answered.

She shifted, wrapping her arms around his middle and pulling herself against him. Her warmth seeped into him, melting the cold wall he tried so desperately to build around his heart.

"How long have we been asleep?" she asked, yawning.

"About an hour or so, I'd guess."

The rain had stopped, the air tinged with the clean smell of a tropical washing. The late afternoon sun shone on the front of the shack, its rays slowly dropping by the minute.

They had a few hours before dark, though. And despite knowing they should head back, he wasn't quite ready yet.

She stretched and he watched her glorious body unfold before his eyes. Her voluptuous breasts thrust upward, begging for his hands and his mouth. Then she settled against him again, as if she trusted him to take care of her.

Fuck if that wasn't exactly what he wanted to do.

"Michael, what happened earlier was —"

He placed a finger on her lips to silence her. Right now he couldn't bear to hear her speech about what had just happened between them. "Don't talk right now. I need you again."

Moisture glistened in her eyes and she blinked back tears. Damn the woman was emotional.

Who was he kidding? He was worse than her.

Instead of talking about making love, he wanted to do it. The need to drive his cock into her again was the only thing he'd allow himself to think about. Pressing a soft kiss to his lips, she sighed and swept her tongue inside.

The kiss was achingly sweet and he responded, tightening his grip around her and giving back what she gave. A long, drugging kiss, lazy and tender, with a depth that took his breath away.

When she threw her leg across his crotch and scooted her moistened heat against his thigh, his cock responded—hardening, lengthening, as if reaching out for her.

Her head rested on his chest. She swept her hand over his stomach and lower, grabbing hold of him. She squeezed him, stroked him, brought him to life. His balls tightened and strained until he was slowly fucking her hand, completely hard and ready for her.

Despite his need to throw her down and ease his throbbing ache inside her, he held off, letting her play. He enjoyed the feel of her hand on him, its warmth, its strength, the sweet tenderness with which she stroked.

Now that— that he could live with forever.

He stilled, thinking those forbidden thoughts again. Not forever. Right now. Right now, with her hand on his shaft, and what would soon follow. She was like a fire in his blood, but not an eternal flame. A quick spark. And once he'd walked through the fire a few times, the flame would die out.

It had to. There was no other choice.

He bounded off the bed, his body heating at the way her eyes followed the movements of his cock. She licked her lips, and he burned hotter.

Serena sat up. "Let me suck it, Michael."

He bit back the groan that bubbled up in his throat, the thought of her hot, wet mouth surrounding the aching head of his cock more appealing by the second. But right now he had more pressing thoughts.

Something he'd been dying to do since the first day they'd met. Something they'd even talked about earlier.

"Later. Right now I want something else."

She arched a brow, her nipples hardening. He smiled, knowing just the thought of fucking again had fired her up instantly.

With a quick scoot to the edge of the bed she wrapped her arms around his hips, drawing close to his cock. But she only rested her cheek against it, close enough her hot breath sailed over the sensitive head.

"Tell me what you want," she murmured, her voice a soft vibration against his stomach.

He dragged her up against him until she was kneeling on the bed, her breasts pressed against his chest. She wound her arms around his neck, her finger slightly raking against the nape of his neck. He shivered and brought his mouth down over hers.

Like an addict who couldn't get enough of the drug that would be his downfall, he dipped his tongue into her mouth and ravaged her lips, trying to crawl inside her so deeply he'd never get free.

Did he even want to?

Once again he shoved the deeper thoughts aside and concentrated on the warm, willing woman in his arms. He ran his hands up the sides of her body, feeling her shudder as his fingertips brushed along the sides of her luscious breasts. She moaned when he pulled back and grazed his palms over her distended nipples.

Dipping his head down he licked first one, then the other nipple, finally fitting his mouth around a swollen, taut bud, rewarded by her gasp of delight. He rolled her nipple around his tongue and she pushed her hips against his crotch, undulating against his rigid cock.

With a quick twist he turned her around, pushing against her upper back so she ended up in a kneeling position on the bed.

He paused and sucked in a breath at the sight of her gorgeous, full ass. Moisture glistened from her pussy lips. She threw her head back, her long blond curls trailing down her back.

If he'd had a camera he could busy himself for the next hour or so taking pictures of the lush vision in front of him. His beautiful goddess was on her knees, ready to take his hard, heavy cock deep inside her dripping pussy.

Every man's dream.

Turning her head to the side, her gaze met his. She smiled. "See anything you like?"

"Oh yeah," he rasped, taking his cock into his hand and stroking it, knowing how much she liked to watch him.

She wriggled her ass at him in response, and bit down on her bottom lip, sucking it into her mouth. His shaft pulsed in his hand.

Enough foreplay. He needed to bury his cock deep inside her, feel her heat surround him, squeeze him until he couldn't hold back any longer.

Positioning her at the edge of the mattress, he pressed against her, grabbing a handful of her full ass cheeks, squeezing them, delighting in her moan of pleasure when the head of his cock probed between her pussy lips.

He teased her for a few minutes, rubbing against her clit until her juices spilled over his hand and cock.

"Michael, please."

"You know I love it when you beg, baby," he teased.

He leaned in, spreading her outer lips and eased inside her. He closed his eyes and focused his mind on the sensations of her pussy closing around him, pulling him inside

She moaned when he was fully inside, and he allowed her a few minutes to adjust. Besides, if he didn't move he could feel every one of the contractions that clenched his shaft.

His hands swept over her ass cheeks until he found her hips. Then he pulled back a little and thrust lightly against her, not fully penetrating. Her breathing increased to slow pants and she backed into him.

Fuck, that was intense. He pulled out again, then thrust hard, shoving his cock in to the hilt.

She whimpered. "Oh, God Michael, that's so good."

"Oh, yeah," he groaned. He could come instantly if he wanted to. His cock pulsed with the strain of holding back. But he knew she enjoyed this as much as he, and he wanted to prolong the pleasure— make it good for her, too.

His fingers bit into her hips as he ground his cock deeply within her, pulling back repeatedly and shoving it in as far as it would go. Once they got a tempo going, he rode her hard and fast, adjusting to her body signals, knowing when she wanted it harder, sensing when he needed to ease up.

The pleasure was intense, more than he could have expected. The visual of her ass pumping hard against him nearly had him coming in screaming agony. But he held off, stopped when he felt the pulsing contractions tighten his balls. He had to last awhile longer.

But Serena wouldn't have any of his hesitance. She leaned forward then backed against him, slapping her ass against him, hard.

He'd never experienced anything as erotic as this. "Oh, yeah baby, fuck me."

Her wet pussy slid easily against his shaft, her juices pouring over his balls. He knew she was getting close by the pulsing contractions as her pussy squeezed his cock relentlessly.

"Fuck me harder," she moaned.

Eager to please her, he stepped up his thrusts. Grabbing a handful of her hair he tugged, her head tilting back, her animal grunts spurring him on.

"You like me riding you like this, baby?" he asked, focusing on her pleasure, the feel of her fucking back against him.

"Yes. Harder, Michael, harder."

He leaned back and pummeled her, slamming his rod so hard inside her his balls slapped her pussy. She gasped and cried out, bucking back against him in wild abandon.

His balls tightened up against him. "Fuck my cock, baby," he rasped, feeling the first contractions overwhelm him.

Arching her back she let out a low moan followed by cries of ecstasy as she came all over his cock, clenching him so tightly the sensations sent him over the edge. His release hit at the same time and he thrust once more, burying his cock as far as it would go as he pumped his hot come into her.

The spasms continued nonstop, stealing his breath, forcing him to hold tight to her hips until he had no more to give. He collapsed on top of her back, wrapping his arms around her waist and holding her as close to him as he could.

Dizziness overcame him. He was mindless, incapable of coherent thought or words. The orgasm had drained him both physically and mentally. When she dropped down on the mattress he slipped off and pulled her close to him, his hands roaming over her sweat soaked skin.

The scent of sex permeated the air, mixing with the smell of rain and her sweet scent, intoxicating him, lulling him into restful peace.

Never before had he been so caught up in the frenzy of fucking, only to follow up with a contented relaxation. Holding Serena in his arms seemed as natural as breathing. With other women he fucked them and when it was over he jumped out of bed and went back to his normal life.

With Serena, all he wanted was to be with her, hold her, inhale her scent. And once they got out of bed, he actually wanted to talk to her.

He swept his hands over her body as if he owned every square inch of her, delighting at the goose bumps popping out on her skin when he lightly trailed his fingers over her spine. She giggled when he cupped her ass cheeks and slipped his finger in the crevice there.

Despite knowing he should get up and drag them out of there, he couldn't quite fit his mind around any movement. Instead, he was content to hold her in his arms.

He never wanted to let her go.

Drowsy, he yawned, his thoughts centered on the spectacular woman who'd given everything to him.

She was amazing, he thought, his eyelids suddenly feeling heavy.

She was his.

"I love you Serena," he murmured, then sighed and drifted off.

Chapter Eleven

ß

Michael's words stayed in Serena's head the rest of the night. They were all she thought of. He'd awakened after a short snooze and they'd dressed and headed back to their room for a hot shower and dinner.

Not once had he mentioned telling her he loved her. Nor had she asked him if that's what he'd really said.

Maybe she'd simply dreamed hearing the words she'd spent her lifetime longing to hear from a man.

But to hear it from him? No way. She must have been mistaken.

What if she hadn't heard wrong? What if he had admitted he loved her? How would that change things between them? Should she ask him to repeat himself? Perhaps she could ask him to put it in writing.

Yeah, right. That would be dumb. She rolled her eyes and imagined that conversation. She'd heard wrong. It was as simple as that. After all, when they'd returned to their suite, he'd bid her a quiet goodnight and gone to his room.

He hadn't asked her to sleep with him, hadn't held her in his arms all night long like she'd wanted him to, nor had he made love to her again.

She sighed and finished making breakfast, putting the eggs and bacon on their plates as soon as she heard Michael's bedroom door open. Her heart thrummed against her chest at the sight of him, each day bringing her closer to the knowledge that she'd fallen hopelessly in love with him.

And with every passing day the thought that their interlude was quickly coming to an end filled her with dread.

Unless she was wrong about that. Unless the declaration of love she thought she'd heard yesterday had, in fact, been real. She made up her mind to ask him—not knowing would drive her crazy. At least if she knew, one way or the other, she could either discuss their options for the future, or steel her heart against breaking when the time came to leave.

"Morning," she said brightly, placing their plates on the balcony and pouring a cup of coffee for Michael.

"Morning," he said softly, his expression wary.

Had he already realized his mistake? Was he looking for a way to backpedal from what he'd said?

"Sleep well?" she asked.

"Fine."

Dammit, this wasn't going well at all. They were back to square one, tiptoeing around each other like they'd been at the very beginning. Serena felt the loss of intimacy they'd shared, and didn't know what to do to get it back. After yesterday, this should be a time when they felt warm and comfortable around each other, not tense.

"What's on tap for today?" he asked between mouthfuls of egg.

"Um, not sure." They'd missed Simply Sex yesterday, although what they'd shared had been anything but simple. She rose to grab their schedule.

"Group Sex," she said, then frowned.

He raised a brow and grinned. "Sounds fun."

She looked up from the schedule to meet his hot gaze. This event included sex with other people. Swapping. Anything goes in a group format.

Less than a week ago it had sounded adventurous, thrilling, something she longed to try.

Today, it sounded like a really bad idea. She didn't want to have sex with anyone but Michael. Not today.

Quite possibly never.

But it appeared he was all gung ho over the idea, leading her to believe that she'd been mistaken in what she heard him say yesterday. Either that or they had completely differing views on what love meant.

Her appetite disappeared. She pushed the eggs around on her plate and took a few nibbles of bacon. Michael wolfed down his food as if he hadn't been fed in days.

No loss of appetite on his side, apparently.

Finally, she couldn't stand it. Good or bad, she had to know.

"Michael, I need to ask you a question."

He stopped, his fork midway to his mouth. "Yeah?"

"About yesterday…"

She saw him swallow, hard. Knew it then, even before she asked the question.

"What about it?"

"You said you loved me."

He looked at his plate and put the fork down, then grabbed his coffee and took a long swallow. Serena could swear she saw sweat bead on his upper lip. And were his hands shaking?

Why was the subject of love like a death sentence to men? She'd never understood that one. Not when she'd desperately searched her entire life for someone she could be compatible with—intellectually as well as sexually. And she'd found him, only to find him having a near breakdown at her mention of the "L" word.

"Never mind." She didn't want to know. Screw knowing. And screw him, too. She rose and took her plate to the kitchen. Michael followed.

"Wait. I want to answer your question."

She slipped the plate into the dishwasher and turned, leaning her hip against the counter. Crossing her arms, she said, "Go ahead."

He shifted on the balls of his feet like a kid who'd been caught with his hand in the cookie jar. Honestly.

"I said it, but it didn't mean what you thought it meant."

Oh, that was a good lie. "I see."

"No, I don't think you do."

She crossed her arms and got comfortable. This should be good. "Then why don't you explain it to me."

"Yesterday was…fantastic. Tremendous. The best day I'd had in a long time. I think you know that as well as I do."

She felt herself warm, despite her rising irritation still remembering the way they'd come together, the way his cock had felt buried to the hilt inside her. "Yes, it was nice."

"Well, with a guy, we sometimes mistake rousing passion for love, and say something stupid."

Now she was getting even more heated, only it was a warm blush firing her furnace this time. "Stupid. Like "I love you Serena?" Stupid like that you mean?"

He jammed his hand through his dark locks and blew out a breath. "Something like that, yeah."

"So, you didn't mean you loved me when you told me you loved me."

"Right."

"It just meant 'gee baby, that was a great fuck,' right?"

He scrunched his eyes shut and grimaced, then opened them. She refused to believe the regret she saw reflected in the pools of blue. "Not quite like that."

"No, it's exactly like that. Fine. I felt the same way. It was the best fuck I've ever had. So far this week." Leaving it at that she pushed away from the counter. Slipping past him, she made sure their bodies didn't touch.

"Hey, Serena. Come on." He trailed after her, following her into her bedroom.

She turned abruptly, blocking his further entry into the one place she could garner some privacy. "I need to be alone."

He sighed. "Look, I'm sorry. Damn me and my blurting. I never meant to hurt you."

"Hurt me? You didn't hurt me. Confused me, yes, but hurt me? I'd have to care about you for you to hurt me. I'd have to love you for those words to stab at me. And I don't. I don't care about you, nor do I love you. Today isn't any different than five days ago when we met. Great fucking and no emotional attachment."

His eyes darkened. "Are you sure that's what we are?"

"Positive," she said, ignoring the ache of loss streaming through her. She'd been so stupid, so damn naïve. But not anymore. Now she saw things clearly. "We're great bed partners, Michael. We fuck well together. Let's just keep it at that for the rest of the time, and neither of us will get hurt. Okay?"

She didn't buy his hurt look for a second.

"Fine," he said, his teeth clenched. "If that's the way you want to play it. I'll meet you at five for some fucking great group sex."

He turned on his heel and stormed off. She slammed the bedroom door and threw herself on the bed, damning the tears that welled in her eyes, damning him for making her care, and damning herself for involving her heart in what should have been a week filled with physical pleasure.

She fought the tears, refusing to baby herself. Then, angry at feeling anything at all for someone who so clearly didn't deserve it, she washed her face and chose her outfit for the next activity.

Femme fatale was in order, she thought. She wanted to allure some of the more attractive men, or couples, or whoever it was she'd attract in a group sex environment.

She chose a black dress, skin tight, short, with laces between her breasts.

Spiked heel shoes, and a skimpy black and silver thong. She left her hair long and flowing down her back and spritzed on a tiny bit of perfume, did her makeup and applied "fuck me red" lipstick.

Gazing at her reflection in the mirror, she smiled. Perfect. She'd dressed perfectly for the part she'd play. She looked like a seductress, a siren, a woman who knew exactly what she wanted, who'd demand satisfaction.

If this getup didn't generate her some group action, nothing would. She'd show Michael Donovan who was desirable. She'd have men crawling at her feet to lick her toes tonight, begging for a chance to fuck her. And fuck her they would. She'd have as many as she wanted — maybe even more than one at a time.

And she'd make Michael watch. Not touch her, just watch her come over and over and over again with different men.

He didn't want her. Fine. Others would.

Straightening her shoulders, she inhaled a breath of courage and strolled slowly into the living room.

Michael was there, his back to her. Her heart pinged in her chest at the sight of him in black shorts and white tank top. Casual, yet so incredibly handsome that merely looking at him fired heat between her legs, her panties damp. Her nipples pebbled against the stretchy tight dress. More the better, she thought. He could see that she was ready for action.

"You ready for a little action?" she said.

He turned and his eyes darkened before he had a chance to hide his reaction with a frown. "Yeah, I'm ready."

Okay, he may not love her, but she sure as hell turned him on. And that she could play with. "Let's go."

"Anxious are you?"

She smiled as she stepped out the door in front of him, then grabbed his arm as he moved alongside her. "Very. I've never had group sex before. Just the thought of fucking a bunch of strangers makes me wet."

He arched a brow, and a tic pulsed in his temple. "Does it now?"

She nodded, playing her femme fatale role to the hilt. "Of course. It's the ultimate fantasy, don't you think?"

Shrugging, he kept his eyes straight ahead. "Sounds like fun to me."

They walked the rest of the way in silence. Serena struggled to balance on the stilt-like shoes. Not quite the same as running around in flat sandals or even regular heels. But these made her legs stand out. And she wanted everything about her to stand out tonight.

They arrived to a packed house. Morgan, the resort manager, greeted them and showed them in. Serena was surprised to see her, and commented to that effect.

Morgan laughed, a lilting sound almost like a soft song. "I try to stay in the background and let the guests have a good time."

"Don't you participate?" Serena asked, accepting a glass of wine from one of the waiters.

"Oh, no. This is my job. The adventures are for the paying customers."

Serena recognized the loneliness reflected in Morgan's sapphire eyes. She'd seen it enough in her own mirror. Wants and needs unfulfilled. Morgan quickly masked it with a bright smile, and excused herself to greet other guests.

Milling about the room, Serena evaluated potential sex partners. There were about thirty people present, plenty to choose from. Various ages and shapes and sizes, she made eye contact with a few of the men, satisfied when they smiled and nodded in her direction.

She might not have a ton of actual sexual experience, but she recognized interest on a man's face. Several of the men in the room were definitely interested. Some not half bad looking, either. Even if they weren't six-foot-two with hair like midnight and eyes like the ocean.

They were men. They had cocks. They wanted to fuck. That's all she needed.

Despite the niggling discomfort settling in her stomach, she was bound and determined to enjoy what she'd paid for — some sexual adventure. She hadn't come here to fall in love, and she wouldn't leave without getting her money's worth of eroticism.

* * * * *

Michael tried to remain as inconspicuous as possible under the circumstances, preferring to spend his time keeping an eye on Serena rather than scouting potential sex partners.

He'd blown it. Big time. Blurting out that he loved Serena had changed their entire relationship. Hell, it had changed his feelings.

Despite what he'd told her, he *had* really meant it. He did love her. And that realization scared the living shit out of him. Which was why he'd told her what he had, made up the lame excuse that all men said shit like that.

He'd hurt her. He could tell from the way the blood drained from her face, the way her hands shook despite the front she'd put on. And he had damn good hearing, too. He'd heard her sniffles from behind her bedroom door, and ached to comfort her, to take her in his arms and tell her he'd lied, that he did have feelings for her.

But what purpose would that have served? Telling her how he really felt would only have prolonged the inevitable.

When the week ended, they ended.

And tonight? Damn he didn't want to do this. Not with her, not like this. The thought of another guy touching her filled him with jealousy.

You're a number one prick, Donovan. You don't want her, and you don't want anyone else to have her either. But she made her own choices, and she'd chosen this. And he was shit out of luck. He'd just have to grin and bear it.

Well, he didn't feel like grinning. And he didn't want her to bare it.

Laughing pathetically at his own pun, he downed another glass of champagne and searched out Serena.

She mingled through the crowd like a beauty contestant, smiling and introducing herself to some of the men. Michael steamed at the lecherous glances she received from some of the guys, and even a few of the women.

With any other woman this would be a wild night of debauched fucking, something he'd certainly be up for. But it wasn't just any other woman, it was Serena. And he didn't want anyone else to touch her.

Michael groaned and searched out another glass of champagne. When he found it he downed it in one gulp and wiped the remnants from his lips.

"You're sure putting it away tonight."

Her smile didn't quite reach her eyes. "I'm thirsty."

She pursed her lips and nodded. "Whatever takes the edge off, I guess."

They stood together in silence, watching people mill around. Inevitably, one approached them.

An attractive couple, both in their early thirties, sidled up next to them. They introduced themselves as Jeanine and Rafael.

The woman was tall, built like a brick shithouse, and made up like a Parisian whore. The guy was smarmy and sweaty and looked like a thug.

Michael looked to Serena, whose eyes widened in panic. Michael couldn't help the smile that curled his lips as he politely declined sex with the couple.

Two other couples approached them. Both times, Serena gave him eye signals that clearly indicated she wanted no part of sex with that particular person or couple.

Groups began to pair off, the sounds of sex growing throughout the darkened room. Groans of pleasure and lots of heavy breathing permeated the place.

And yet Serena hadn't seemed too interested in getting down and dirty with anyone who had approached them. And Michael sure as hell wasn't going to make any suggestions. In fact, he'd be happy as hell if they turned around and walked out.

"You ready to go?" he suggested.

"Why?"

"It's obvious you don't really want to do this. Why don't we get the hell out of here and go back to our room."

With a defiant lift of her chin, she said, "Who says I don't want to do this?"

"I do. You've turned down every guy who's approached you."

"They were icky."

He hid his smile behind his glass of champagne, emptying it and setting it on a nearby table. "Let's go, Serena."

When he took her arm she wrenched it away. She half twisted toward a man standing nearby and tapped him on the shoulder. When the man turned, Michael groaned. This one was right up Serena's alley. Tall, tanned, athletic body—fucking perfect. And the woman with him was, too. Slender and fine boned with dark exotic eyes and raven hair that fell midway down her back.

Any other time a woman like that would have him hard in an instant, raring to fuck. But this wasn't any other time. And the woman wasn't Serena.

The guy graced Serena with a bright, even smile and introduced himself as Sam.

Serena took one look at Michael, then turned back to Sam and said, "How about it, Sam? You want to fuck?"

Chapter Twelve

** SO**

Sam grinned. "Hell yeah, honey. I'll fuck you. Let's get to it."

Serena swallowed, her throat suddenly gone dry. So much for bravado. Now that she was faced with the prospect of fucking this stranger, she no longer had the stomach for it.

In fact, she might seriously have to give some thought to throwing up.

But this is why she'd come to Paradise Resort. The erotic adventure of a lifetime, a chance to experience everything she'd fantasized about, and knew she wouldn't be able to living in a small town.

So, buck it up, girlie. Get your ass to wiggling and fuck that big boy in front of you.

Sam trailed his hand up her bare arm, and she shivered. But not the same way Michael made her shiver. She was revolted by the concept of engaging in sex with this stranger. And the way his partner was leering at her led her to believe she'd be doing a two woman, one man, three way. Oh sure, she enjoyed watching videos with two women together, especially if the man participated, but this woman did nothing for her libido.

Oh hell. No one did anything for her libido except the man she loved.

The one who looked pissed as hell right now, whose eyes darkened, whose nostrils flared.

"That's enough," he said, and yanked Sam's hand off her arm. Serena breathed a sigh of relief as Sam walked away with a shrug.

"Michael, I—" she started to explain what had happened, that she'd changed her mind, but never got the chance. He roughly grabbed her arm and dragged her into the throng of bodies in the now darkened sex room. She tripped over piles of shoes and clothing, the smell of sex filling the air around her. She glanced down and saw two men with their hands and mouths all over a naked woman. One fucked her from behind, the other rammed his long cock down her throat.

Moist desire seeped between her legs despite her panic. Where was he taking her? Was he so angry that he was going to force her to participate in sex with another man? Or maybe he'd spotted another woman, and wanted to take two of them at once. She'd never considered there might be something in this for him.

That was it, she thought miserably. She was going to be forced to partake of a three way that she had no interest in. She'd have to watch as Michael fucked another woman, took that woman to the same heights of pleasure he'd taken her.

What was she going to do? Complain? No, she refused to do that. This whole thing had been her idea anyway. And then tonight she'd hit him upside the head with her enthusiasm for group sex. She was just getting what she deserved.

Finally, he stopped. They were near the wall in the center of the room. Couples fucked all around them—pairs, threesomes, even foursomes. Some were two women together, some were two men. Anything was acceptable at Paradise Resort.

She turned to face him but he gripped her arms and flipped her around.

"Turn around and watch," he said, holding on to her arms as he stood behind her. "This is what you wanted, right?"

She took a deep breath and nodded. "Yes, this is what I wanted."

"Is there anyone in this room you want to fuck?"

She refused to answer.

"Tell me," he growled, sweeping her hair to the side and biting the nape of her neck, hard.

She moaned despite her vow not to let him get to her. The slightest touch and she was like a panting bitch around him. Her nipples stiffened and she ached between her legs — damp, moist and desperate for what only he could provide. But she would not relent, would not tell him how she felt.

Despite her efforts to wrench free, he held her still, pressing against her, enough that she felt his hard shaft against her ass cheeks, knew this whole thing made him as hot as she was.

"Answer me," he said hotly, his fingers squeezing the tender flesh of her arms. "Tell me who you want to fuck."

He bit down on her neck again, then reached around her and yanked the laces open on her dress. Her breasts spilled into his hands and he squeezed them, pinching her nipples until she cried out in a painful pleasure unlike anything she'd experienced yet.

"You, dammit! I want to fuck you!"

She heard his exhalation of breath, his aroused panting against her neck. With one forceful thrust he ripped the dress off her shoulders and yanked it down until she was bare from the waist.

"I can't give you what you want," he said.

Already knowing that, she nodded. "I know. I don't care. I just want whatever we can have for the time we have left."

"Then I'll make it so damn good you'll never forget it."

Soft candlelight flickered around the room, showcasing an erotic display of tangled limbs and naked bodies engaged in various sex acts. The sweet smell of arousal tinged the air with a sexual electricity that flamed her desire. Coupled with the fact that Michael was viciously stripping her naked and her legs shook so fiercely she could barely stand.

He pulled the dress down her legs and she stepped out of it, leaving her wearing only her thong panties and spiked heels. Michael tangled his hand in her hair and pulled her roughly against him. Sometime during the frenzy of stripping he'd removed his shirt, the crisp hairs on his chest grazing her back.

She heard the rustle of clothing as he slipped his shorts off, felt the hard tip of his cock nestle against the silk of her panties.

"These have to go," he said tightly, once again shredding her panties with a vicious yank. She mentally calculated the cost of two pairs of expensive panties, now shredded and useless.

She didn't care—loved his fierce, erotic, anything goes nature, needed his passion as much as she needed everything else about him. Despite her vow to stay uninvolved, she finally faced her denial.

She was in love with Michael, and could do nothing to stop the whirlwind of emotions that feeling brought about. And now she didn't care. She wanted him like she'd never wanted another man before, like she knew she'd never want another man after. And she'd take whatever remaining time they had together, with no expectations for a future.

"You don't want to fuck anyone else?" he whispered against her ear.

"No. Just you."

"Then, fuck me," he said, pushing her forward until she had to grasp the railing in front of her. Her ass jutted out behind her and Michael stepped between her spread legs.

"You look hot like this," he rasped. "Your legs spread, those *fuck me* shoes making your legs look long and sexy, your pussy open so anyone walking by can see."

She felt the juices pour from her, heard the moans escape her lips when he reached down and caressed her dripping snatch, sliding his fingers gently inside and pumping once, twice, three times.

"Fuck my fingers," he commanded, his voice as black as the darkness of the room. "Show me how much you want my cock."

Eagerly she bucked back against his hand, sliding her wet pussy over his fingers, moaning when he reached around with his other hand and found her clit. He circled the sensitive nub, relentless in his quest to bring her pleasure.

"Stop, please," she begged. "You're going to make me come."

He withdrew his fingers and replaced them with his hard cock, the head probing her slit until he found the opening. With one hard thrust he entered her.

She screamed loudly then bit down on her lip, hoping she wouldn't draw the gazes of the crowd surrounding her, but no one paid attention. They were all engaged in their own erotic play, mindless to the goings on around them. Once in awhile someone would change partners. Serena wondered if they knew who they were fucking, or even if they cared.

She cared, she realized. She cared who she fucked. It was either going to be Michael or no one. Her mind and body awash in the sensations of this one man, she vowed to etch each moment into her memories to last her a lifetime.

With every thrust he pushed her forward, hard. Serena grasped the railing with her hands and held tight, her legs planted. Michael leaned forward and grasped her breasts, held them in his hands as he stroked her relentlessly.

"This stuff exciting enough for you?" he growled. "Fucking while other people fuck and suck all around you?"

The exciting part was Michael's cock buried inside her. He was the only thing that mattered. "Yes," she lied, building the protective shield around her heart. "Yes, it excites me."

He let go of her breasts, one hand reaching down between her legs to stroke her clit. He thrummed the sensitive nub repeatedly. Coupled with the delightful sensations of his cock ramming hard against her, she felt the first stirrings of her orgasm. Revving up her own thrusts she pushed back against him, rewarded with his grunt of pleasure.

"You ready to come baby?" he whispered against her ear, increasing the thrumming of her clit with relentless accuracy.

Unable to speak she could only nod and then shudder as the first wave of contractions washed over her. Gripping the railing tight she pushed against his cock, lifted her head and howled wildly, not caring at all who heard or watched.

At the same time Michael grunted in her ear and slammed his hard shaft home, his balls slapping against her clit. She felt the spurts of his come jettison inside her and ground her ass against him.

They were perfect together. Her body had been made for his. He was the only one to bring her to such incredible heights of pleasure, stimulating her in ways she'd never thought possible.

He withdrew and she relaxed her grip on the railing. He turned her around, cradling her in his arms. She smiled into his chest, feeling a contentment she knew was fleeting. While her breathing returned to normal, she held on to him tight, knowing that the time for them was slowly slipping away.

* * * * *

Protect. The first word that came to Michael's mind was protect. Wasn't that what he'd been doing for almost a week now? Protecting Serena from the types of men who would take advantage of her in a place like this?

He tightened his hold on her, his hands slipping down her back to cup her ass and pull her against him. A woman like her had no place in a resort like this. She was too naïve, too trusting.

Hell, she'd trusted him, and look what he was doing to her. Hurting her, leading her on, letting her feel something for him, only to rip the rug out from under her with his lies.

"You okay?" he asked, hating that he'd even care enough to know.

She nodded against his chest. "Fine," she murmured in a contented purr.

Protect. Shit. He was so fucked where this woman was concerned. He'd fallen in love with her and knew that he'd let her go anyway. Stupid, stupid, stupid. How could he let someone like her slip through his fingers? Did he think women like Serena stood around waiting for dumbasses like him to pick them up?

This could be his last chance at happiness, and he was too damn shell-shocked to do anything about it. He'd let his bad experience with his ex-wife color every decision he made about women.

Rightly so. He had his own heart to protect.

"Let's get dressed and get out of here." He gathered her clothes and helped her dress, refusing to touch her. What he really wanted to do was hold her tight against him, feel every inch of her skin cover him. But it was time to start letting go.

After they returned to their room, Serena went to take a shower, seemingly confused over his lack of conversation. Michael stepped into his own steamy shower and leaned against the cool tile wall, hoping the pummeling water would beat some sense into him.

They had one day left. One day, and then she'd be gone.

He stepped out of the shower and dried off, then went to find her.

She was in the kitchen fixing them a snack. Wearing plain cotton shorts and a t-shirt, her hair damp and streaming down her back, she looked completely different from the sex siren who'd tantalized him tonight with her wriggling ass and shapely legs.

Without makeup she looked like a college girl herself, not a professor. A down-home Kansas girl with a simple beauty that took his breath away.

"Hungry?" she asked, bringing out a tray with sandwiches and fresh vegetables.

"Starving."

She set the tray on the table in front of the sofa and went back to the kitchen, returning with two glasses of iced tea. "Sex makes me hungry," she said with a smile as she curled up on the couch.

He remembered not too long ago when she'd said she didn't know if sex made her hungry or not. Apparently, it did. "I know the feeling."

They tore into their food, eating as ravenously as they made love.

Correction—fucked. Making love was something you did with a person you cared about. He wouldn't care about her. He'd just fuck her until he couldn't fuck her any more.

Could he be any more ambiguous about this whole thing? He shook his head, amazed at his own lack of decision.

"What's wrong?" she asked, taking a long swallow of tea.

"Nothing. Just thinking about this week."

"It's been wonderful, Michael. Have I thanked you for all you've done for me?"

Oh sure. Pile on the guilt. What had he done, other than toy with her emotions and tell her he loved her, only to take it back like a bully on the school playground? "No thanks necessary. I've enjoyed it."

She set her tea on the table and turned serious eyes on him. "I need to ask you a favor."

"Okay, shoot."

Sucking in her bottom lip in a way he found incredibly sexy, she hesitated for a second before saying, "We have two nights left together."

"Right."

"I'd like to sleep with you. In your bed."

Oh, shit. "Why?" he blurted.

She arched a brow. "I don't know, exactly. Call it a need, or something indefinable. I just feel a need to sleep in your arms at night."

Protect. That word swirled around his head until he wanted to shake it out. Violently, if necessary. Sleeping with her would be intimate. Personal. Emotional.

As if she sensed his hesitation, she placed her hand on his knee. "I know how you feel, if you're worried about that. I know you don't want to be involved with me beyond this week. I can accept that. Consider this just another adventure for me. And you promised to help make this week exciting for me, didn't you?"

That he did. He'd made it exciting all right. Exciting, erotic, and completely disastrous.

So sleeping with her would nearly kill him, so what? Just what he deserved for leading her on in the first place. "Yes, we can sleep together."

"Thank you."

Michael tried to concentrate on work, putting the finishing pieces on his plotline for the next book. Serena sat with him, as he'd grown accustomed to, offering ideas and listening to him throw out suggestions.

She was amazingly insightful where his work was concerned, thinking along the same lines as he with character development and plotline. He could use her as an assistant, because he never had anyone to talk to about his writing.

After tomorrow, he wouldn't have her to talk to, either.

He'd miss that. A lot.

When she began to yawn, he closed the laptop and grabbed her hand, pulling her up beside him. "Let's go to bed."

She nodded and offered a sleepy smile, following him into his bedroom.

They undressed and slid into bed together. Serena snuggled up against him and laid her head on his shoulder, her hand draped across his chest. Michael stared at the ceiling, ignoring how perfect she felt in his arms. Ignoring how much he wanted to pull her under him and make love to her all night long.

"Thank you for doing this," she said.

"It's no big deal, Serena. Really."

"It is to me."

And that's what made this whole scenario suck.

"Night," she murmured in a sleepy voice.

"Night."

When the sounds of her rhythmic breathing indicated she was asleep, Michael exhaled.

In his bed, in his arms, was exactly where Serena belonged. How in the hell was he ever going to let her go?

Chapter Thirteen

ᗡᑕ

Waking up in Michael's arms had been heaven, everything she'd dreamed of. Serena had slept well for the first time all week.

Spending her last day stretched out on the beach, her body warmed by the tropical sun, she smiled, thinking about every new experience she'd had this week.

She was twenty-eight years old and had never spent all night snuggled in a man's arms. The few relationships she'd had did not include the guy sleeping over. In fact, the thought hadn't even occurred to her.

But with Michael, she'd wanted to sleep with him since the very first day. And now she had. With still one more night to come.

And one more day of erotic pleasure to share together.

She pushed aside the relentless ache in her middle at the thought that today was their last day together. From now on she'd live in the present, concerned only with the here and now. Not the 'later' that she couldn't change, anyway.

Michael didn't want her. Pure and simple. She didn't have what it took to make a long-term relationship work. She'd thought about this a lot, and chalked it up to her inexperience with men. Without the first idea how to form a lasting relationship, she'd gone about it all wrong.

Nothing to do about it now, except enjoy the day.

"I brought you one of those frou frou drinks that women like."

Serena shielded her eyes from the sun and looked up at Michael. "Frou frou drinks?"

"Yeah. Pina colada. With fruit and an umbrella."

She sat up and accepted the frothy concoction from him, arching a brow. "Do I look like a frou frou drink kind of woman?"

He tilted his head as if examining her for the frou frou gene. She punched his arm. "Stop."

"Sorry. You don't like it?" he asked, his lips curled in a generous smile.

She took a sip and licked her lips. "Yummy, actually. Smooth and creamy. Kind of like that sweet cream that comes from your cock."

Eyes darkening, he said, "Careful. You might get ravaged right here on the beach, in front of all these people."

She waved her hand. "I've had sex in front of groups before. Old hat stuff to me. Give it your best shot."

"Don't tempt me. Besides, I'm waiting for later."

Her body tingled at the thought of today's event—their last together, and the one she'd been anticipating all week. The Private Cove for Two. No crowds, no indoor rooms, just the two of them, outside, on the beach, in their own palace of erotic joys.

"I can't wait," she said, trailing her fingertip along the line of his strong jaw. She'd miss the feel of his stubble scratching against her skin.

They snuggled together in the sun, Serena content to lie by Michael's side. They read, they swam, they even engaged in some beach volleyball with some of the other guests. Before long it was time to get ready for their adventure.

After a quick shower to rinse off the suntan lotion, Serena dressed and she and Michael headed to the beach.

The Private Cove was on a secluded section of beach off limits to any guest other than the ones scheduled for the day. A sultan's tent stood in the center of the beach, its fabric sides and waving flags undulating in the soft, warm breeze.

Morgan greeted them, the soft ocean breeze blowing her red hair behind her. In her blue sarong she looked like a mermaid swept in from the sea.

Serena wondered why a gorgeous woman like her lived such a lonely existence on an island like this, and didn't even partake of the pleasures the resort offered.

"Welcome to the Private Cove," Morgan said in her typically husky voice. "I think you'll both enjoy this experience."

She led them inside. Oversized pillows were strewn over a bed draped in silks and satins in jeweled colors. Two rooms on either side of the bed contained their outfits for the day. Middle Eastern music filled the room with sensual, seductive sounds.

"Indulge yourselves in unlimited pleasures." Morgan pointed to a tray filled with fruits, cheeses and drink. "More will be delivered, discreetly of course, later on."

After Morgan bid them farewell, Serena and Michael headed to their respective changing rooms.

Serena giggled as she fastened the gold medallion belt around her belly, then inserted the green emerald in her navel. A harem dancer. Thrilled at the prospect of tantalizing Michael to the brink of madness, she slipped on the sheer emerald harem pants and turned to the mirror.

Perfect. She'd swept her hair high on top of her head in a long ponytail, and fastened the matching green veil behind her ears, covering the lower half of her face. The bra was made entirely of gold sequins, showing off a generous amount of cleavage. The pants hung low at her waist, the belt slung over the top. A gold sequined thong was visible through the sheer harem pants.

After slipping on the gold, snake-shaped armbands, she stepped out of the dressing area to find Michael standing before her, looking for all the world like a sexy sultan.

His chest bare, he wore only a black brocade vest, which hung open to reveal a gold medallion hung on a long, thick chain. The billowy sultan pants he wore complemented the vest and made him look like a sexy, rugged genie. The only other accoutrements to his outfit were the two golden armbands clasped tight around his bulging biceps.

He was so damn hot he stopped her heart.

"Wow," was all she could manage.

"I feel stupid," he said. He stood there, legs spread, hands on hips, looking for all the world like the commanding sultan. "You look sexy as hell."

Her body started its familiar rush of anticipation as she lowered her head in a bow. "Your slave for the day, master."

He arched a brow. "Slave, eh? Come here then, woman."

She fought back the smile. Slaves did not giggle at their sultans. With a slow saunter, making sure she wiggled her hips suggestively, she approached him.

"I believe you will entertain me today," he commanded.

"As you wish, my master." The thought of being subservient to his every wish tantalized her, teased her with a promise of sensual delights. "What is your pleasure?"

His blue eyes darkened. "You are my pleasure," he whispered, caressing her bare arm with his knuckles.

She shivered and inhaled a shaky breath.

"Dance for me, slave."

Her throat went dry at the thought of dancing for Michael. But she so wanted to please him today, determined to give him an experience he would never forget.

"Sit. Let me entertain you."

He slipped onto the bed and lay prone, propped up on one elbow. His dark eyes never left her, gazing appreciatively over her body. Serena stood at the edge of the bed and inhaled, hoping she wouldn't come off looking like a complete fool.

She let the music take over, its slow, seductive tones filling her mind and body with images of sensual pleasure, and began to move, communicating without words her desire for Michael.

Michael sucked in a breath at the sight before him. As if the sexy as hell harem outfit she wore wasn't enough torture, Serena began to move, slowly undulating her hips and moving her hands gently, as if she were caressing the very air around her.

The gold bra shimmered in the sunlight pouring in through the open drapes of the tent, shining on the swell of her breasts spilling over the top of the garment. The sheer, green harem pants covered nothing. Her silky legs were clearly visible, as was her barely covered pussy.

His cock had been hard since the moment she'd stepped out of the dressing room, her sea green eyes lighting up like emeralds to match the slinky, seductive outfit she wore.

And now, watching her dance before him, she took his breath away. Sweat beaded his brow and he furiously wiped it away, not wanting to miss a moment of her movements.

She was a siren, waving her hands in the air as if to summon the demons of pleasure. Her hips undulated from side to side and she rolled them towards him then back again, teasing him with her actions.

He wanted to rip that sexy getup off her, throw her in the midst of the pillows and lose himself in her.

When she turned her back to him and shook her ass to a quick tempo song, he almost lost it. Without hesitation he reached for his cock and stroked the shaft over his pants, the silk rubbing against the aching head. It felt like Serena's slit, so soft it was almost painful.

"Come here," he said, feeling like he'd been tortured long enough.

She turned and smiled at him through the sheer green veil, and approached the foot of the bed. He bounded off the bed and stood next to her, releasing the veil from her face and tossing it aside.

Her tongue darted out and swept across her full bottom lip. He swallowed and followed her movements, desperately needing to feel her tongue slide across the head of his swollen cock.

Without words he undressed her—slowly, deliberately prolonging the removal of each piece of her clothing, until she stood near naked in front of him. The sequined thong was the only thing remaining and she smiled up at him, obviously remembering his penchant for ripping off her panties. She shook her head.

"These aren't mine. As it is you've destroyed two pair of expensive panties."

"I'll mail you a check," he teased, then carefully pushed the thong down her hips until it pooled at her feet.

She stood gloriously naked before him. His harem girl, his slave, his princess, his siren and seductress. She was the woman of all his dreams and she was his.

For today.

Serena slipped the vest off his shoulders, then dropped to her knees and pulled off his pants. His cock sprung straight out, hard and pulsating.

She smiled and looked up at him, then cradled his balls in her hand and leaned forward to grasp the head of his penis with her lips. With one, long swipe of her tongue she licked the sensitive head. He groaned at the sheer pleasure of her warm, wet mouth, then died a thousand deaths when she sucked him in deep.

"I love sucking your cock," she said after she slipped him out of her mouth to stroke him with her hands. "I love the feel of its satiny texture on my lips and tongue, the salty sweet taste of you that spills out drop by drop."

Obviously, she was trying to kill him, and nearly succeeding. He pulsed in her hands, releasing more droplets which she greedily licked off the head.

He lifted her and pulled her into his arms, delighting in the feel of her breasts crushed against his chest. "You have one sexy mouth."

"Thank you, my master," she said with an impish wink. Staying in character she said, "And now, I wish to offer you a gift."

He arched a brow, not certain of the game she played. "What kind of gift?"

"One I've never given another man." She wound her arms around his neck, sliding her fingers through his hair. Her nails lightly scraped his scalp and he shivered.

"Now I'm interested. Tell me."

With a soft sigh she brought her lips to his and kissed him gently, then pressed her mouth firmly against his, seductively entwining her tongue with his until he felt his legs wobble. He pulled her closer, his hands reaching down to caress that cleft between the cheeks of her ass.

She stood on her tiptoes, giving him free access to probe between her ass cheeks.

"That's what I want, " she said, demurely dropping her gaze.

"What?" He could barely concentrate, his mind and body fixated on stroking that secret place on her behind.

"That. Oh, yes, that."

His eyes widened in shock. Never in a million years had he been prepared for her wanting to be fucked that way.

"Spell it out for me. Tell me what you want."

Her gaze met his and she smiled. "I want you to fuck me in the ass, Michael."

His throat went dry and he struggled for words. Excitement filled his balls, tightening and promising a gut wrenching orgasm. "Are you sure that's what you want?"

She nodded excitedly. "Oh, yes. We've done everything together. I've thought about this a lot. I've, never…"

"Never?"

She shook her head. "No, and I want you to be the first."

Heart pounding against his chest, he considered her request. Okay, he considered it for all of a millisecond before his cock made the decision for him. "I'll make it good for you baby. I promise."

She smiled, her expression so full of trust it humbled him. "I know you will."

He pressed her down on the bed and laid next to her, pulling her against him and kissing her until she whimpered.

He would make this good for her. Make sure she was ready, relaxed and primed for the moment when he'd plunge his hard cock into her delectable ass. Pushing her on her back, he trailed his fingers over the silky softness of her cheeks and down her throat, following with his mouth, licking a line from her jaw to her collarbone.

She shivered and her nipples tightened. He circled the dusky peaks with his fingertips, lightly tapping the tip until it stood upright. Then he covered the peak with his lips, rolling it around on his tongue until she gasped and lifted her hips in an unspoken request.

"Soon, baby, soon," he murmured, delighting in the texture of her skin, so different from his own. She was so soft, so small compared to him that he wanted to cradle her gently. Then again he wanted to fuck her so hard she screamed in painful pleasure.

He chuckled to himself. Nothing like a little contradiction.

Lavishing attention on her breasts, one by one, until she cried out for him to touch her lower, he scooted down her body, blazing a trail with his hands and following it with his tongue.

He laved her flat stomach and tickled her belly button with the tip of his tongue until she giggled, then he moved lower, spreading her legs apart and slipping his hands under her buttocks to lift her delectable mound within his reach.

Inhaling her sweet, musky fragrance, he laid his tongue over her slit and slowly licked upward. She bucked off the bed and gasped. With slow, torturous strokes he licked her up and down, stopping every now and then to insert his tongue into her pussy and lap up her juices.

"Michael, please," she cried, wriggling her hips up and down.

She was ready. Primed. Almost to orgasm.

He sat on his haunches and reached for a condom in the basket on the table next to the bed. Her head on a pillow, she watched his every movement, watched him roll the condom on his aching hard cock, then she smiled at him.

"Tell me to stop if it hurts," he said, not wanting to spoil her pleasure with unbearable pain.

"I will."

Gently, he eased her legs apart and settled between her. She was completely open to his gaze. Her wet slit dripping with juices, that perfect ass puckered and primed for him.

He poured lubricant onto his fingertips and gently probed her ass, watching her for any signs of displeasure. Her breasts rose and fell with each of her deep breaths, but she looked on him in rapt anticipation, lifting her hips and gasping when he inserted one finger into her anus.

Christ, she was so tight. He already knew he'd come fast once he slipped inside her taut hole. Gently he probed, sliding his finger in slowly until it was buried inside her. He felt her tighten around his finger, and began to move it in and out until she grew accustomed to the feel.

While he fucked her ass with his finger he used the thumb of his other hand to circle her clit. Her green eyes glazed over and she whimpered, begging him with nonsensical words to hurry.

"Fuck me, Michael," she cried. "Fuck my ass now."

He slowly pulled his finger out and lubricated his shaft, nestling in between her outstretched legs.

"Touch yourself," he commanded. "Make yourself come while I fuck your ass."

She slid her fingers over her clit and he watched in rapt fascination. Just like the night they'd masturbated for each other. She thrummed her clit and stroked her slit while he placed the head of his cock against her asshole, working the head in gently until it passed the initial barrier and slipped inside her.

Her eyes widened and she gasped. He stilled, waiting for her body to adapt to his size. After a few seconds she began to move against him, urging him further in.

Inch by inch he entered her, until he was buried deep in her tight hole. She breathed in and out through her mouth in panting gasps.

"Are you all right?" he asked.

"Yes," she said. "Just fuck me."

The tempo of her fingers on her clit increased and her ass squeezed him, pulling him in. His balls tightened as he slowly started pumping in and out of her.

"Oh, God, yes," she cried.

He took a forever picture of this scene before him. Serena, her legs drawn up and spread wide open for him, strumming her clit with one hand and pumping two fingers into her pussy with the other. Her tight ass gripped his cock as he thrust deep inside her, burying his shaft all the way in.

Never in his life had he had a moment of such erotic pleasure. He wanted to die, he wanted to come, and he wanted it to last forever.

He thrust repeatedly, his strokes measured and increasing in force and speed as she urged him on, begging him to fuck her faster.

Suddenly, she tensed and lifted her head, her fingers moving faster along her clit.

"I'm coming, Michael," she panted. "Oh, God I'm coming."

He felt the contractions in her ass and she moaned long and low, then let out a scream as she came, furiously pumping her fingers in and out of her pussy. Her head turned from side to side, her hips rising off the bed.

Michael gripped her hips and pushed into her as hard as he could, feeling her ass squeeze him. Juices poured from her pussy onto his cock. He couldn't hold back any longer and thrust furiously, howling in pleasure as he jettisoned a bucket load of come into her ass.

Instantly he withdrew and collapsed on top of her, gathering her close. He felt her shiver.

"You all right?"

"Mmm hmm," she said, holding tight to his arms.

He cradled her against him and kissed the top of her head, overcome with emotion he couldn't put in to words. It was probably best not to say anything anyway. Nothing he said would come out the way he meant it. But he wanted her to know what her gift meant to him, how special it had been.

"I love you Michael," she said.

He stayed silent.

Chapter Fourteen

ഇ

Serena finished packing her things into the suitcase, figuring she'd stalled long enough. No sense putting off the inevitable. Despite longing to stay here in this idyllic fantasy land for the rest of her life, the reality of the end of her adventures intruded harshly into her dreams.

They were due to depart within the hour. She hadn't seen Michael in hours. Soon, she wouldn't see him at all.

Last night had been incredible, the culmination of all her fantasies. Michael had been a tender lover, taking care not to hurt her. Just what she had come to expect from him. He seemed to instinctively know how much she could take — where to draw the line between pleasure and pain.

Afterward, they'd gone back to their room, cleaned up, and spent the remainder of the evening curled up in each other's arms. A bittersweet end to an interlude that Serena would remember the rest of her life.

She had told Michael she loved him. He hadn't responded. Not that she'd expected him to. And yet, she'd wanted him to know. And despite what he'd told her the other day, she knew he felt something for her beyond just sex. But something prevented him from wanting to take it any further.

And who was she to tell him how to feel? If he'd wanted her badly enough, wanted to continue their relationship beyond the boundaries of this fantasy island, he would have said so.

He hadn't. So they'd go their separate ways today, and Serena would tuck the memories of Michael Donovan deep in her heart forever.

With a sigh of resignation she closed her suitcase and stepped into the living room, tugging the wheeled monstrosity behind her. She stepped out onto the balcony for one last look at the turquoise ocean, feel the breeze on her face and smell the salty sweet fragrance of the tropics.

She'd miss this place.

She'd miss Michael more.

* * * * *

Michael jammed the last of his things in his suitcase and snapped it shut, the sound echoing with a finality he didn't want to face.

She loved him. He felt stupid, but he smiled every time he recalled her words. Not that it changed anything. He wasn't someone who had the capacity to love any more. Memories of pain and heartbreak sailed across his memories at the thought of loving someone.

He and his first wife had been a disaster from the start. Oh sure, in his own, typical male ego way, he'd blamed Mari for all the problems in their marriage. But the collapse of their relationship hadn't been entirely her fault. A lot of the blame fell to him. And he realized that he wasn't fit company for a woman to live with, and definitely not to marry.

Because he cared about Serena, he was going to leave her.

Somewhere in that small town in Kansas where she lived was some guy who'd make her happy. Not a used up, cynical, down on love writer like him. He could never give her what she needed.

But until the day he died he'd remember the words she'd uttered after they'd made love. And he'd hold them tight, knowing they were the last words of love anyone would say to him.

She was on the balcony, the vision of her so similar to the one he'd seen that first day. The clothes were different, though. Gone was the dowdy, plain, blousy outfit she'd worn that day they'd met. Instead she wore little black capris, sandals, and a white tube top. Her long hair fell in a single braid down the middle of her back.

When she turned to him and smiled, his heart stopped. He shook his head and smiled back, knowing a day wouldn't go by that he wouldn't think of her and remember her smile, her sweet smell, those green eyes that could light up his heart, and a body he could never tire of.

"You all packed?" she asked.

He nodded. "How about you?"

"Yes."

"When does the new semester begin?" Maybe idle chit chat would pass the time until their departure, force him to think about other things than how much he was going to miss her.

"In three weeks."

He nodded.

"When will you start on your book?"

He shrugged and smiled. "I don't have deadlines. When the impetus strikes I'll crank it out in a month or so."

"Good."

The silence stretched between them, awkward and uncomfortable.

She turned to view the ocean. "I'll miss this place."

"Me too." He'd miss her more. But he wasn't going to say it. Couldn't say it. He wouldn't give her, or him for that matter, unrealistic hope.

"I had a great time, Michael. Thank you for making this an unforgettable experience for me."

He pulled a stray hair away from her face and tucked it behind her ear. "Believe me, Serena, it was my pleasure."

Without hesitation she stepped towards him. He folded his arms around her and rested his chin on her head, trying like hell to keep from begging her to come to California with him.

Which would be a colossal mistake, and would ruin her life.

They separated at the knock on the door. The bellman retrieved their suitcases and told them the shuttle to the airport on the other side of the island was waiting downstairs.

It was better this way, he thought as they followed the bellman downstairs. Better now than three or four months from now when they'd both realize the error they'd made.

This was the best time to say goodbye.

* * * * *

Serena tapped her pencil on the stack on her desk, slipped on her glasses and dug into the pile. Her office looked like a train wreck.

First week of the new semester and she was deluged with paperwork already. Not that she cared. She'd been listless and completely uninterested in anything around her since she'd gotten back from Paradise Resort.

She and Michael had said awkward goodbyes at the airport. A hug, a quick kiss, good luck in the future and that was it. He had walked out of her life forever.

And probably hadn't given her a second thought. Which irritated the hell out of her, much to her surprise.

She *was* unforgettable. She *was* worthy of a man who would traverse the ends of the earth for her. And if Michael Donovan couldn't see that, he could kiss her well-tanned ass.

A little righteous indignation and anger went a long way to soothe a broken heart. It was almost working.

Almost.

In the past month, she'd progressed from thinking about him twenty-four hours a day to merely twenty-two now. She was definitely making headway in that department.

She'd made headway in a lot of areas. Mainly, she refused to hide who she was any longer. Even the men around campus had started to notice her. Most likely due to the fact that she'd tossed out her frumpy clothes and bought some that fit. Stylish, trendy, a tad bit sexy.

She inhaled, enjoying the feel of the satin chemise that slid against her nipples. One of her many new purchases. Along with the black suit she wore today, with its short skirt and fitted jacket. And the to die for pumps that were just a little bit naughty.

Why not? She'd learned a lot about herself at Paradise, and one of the most important things she'd discovered was her sensuality. She was a healthy sexual being. With normal needs and urges that weren't bizarre or unnatural. And some day she'd find a man whose sexual tastes matched her own.

In the meantime, she'd just let them all see how she'd come to life on vacation. And if one of them were ballsy enough to ask her out, then she'd just see what happened.

Right. When hell froze over. The problem was, they might be interested in her, but she wasn't interested in them.

Most likely she never would be. For every time another man would want to touch her, kiss her or make love to her, a tall, tanned hunk with sapphire eyes and a body to die for would cloud her vision.

Face it, Serena. You're fucked. And not in a good way. The man she wanted, the one she loved, was two thousand miles away, living his California life with a bevy of fashion models, and probably hadn't thought about her for one second since they parted ways over a month ago.

"You're all I've thought about for the past month."

Yeah right, she thought, mentally tamping down his voice which permeated her every thought.

"You look gorgeous."

The pencil stilled in her hand and her heart slammed against her chest. No. It couldn't be.

She slipped off her glasses and looked up.

There, leaning in her doorway, looking tanned and handsome in jeans and a white polo shirt, was Michael.

Unable to catch her breath, she couldn't speak. Her legs shook so bad she couldn't stand.

He arched a brow. "Cat got your tongue, Professor?"

"Uh, uh, uh." *Brilliant conversation there, Serena.* "What...what are you doing here?"

With a grin he pushed off from the doorway and walked in the room, then sat on the edge of her desk.

She inhaled his clean, crisp scent which almost brought her to tears. God, she'd missed his smell.

"I had to meet with my editor in New York, so I took a little detour."

"Kansas is quite a detour."

He looked around. "It's a nice detour. Quaint little town."

She snorted. "Yeah, right." He was probably laughing at her quaint little town.

"I'm serious. This is a great place. Talk about a slice of Americana. Reminds me of where I grew up in central California."

That revelation shocked her. "You grew up in a small town?"

He grinned. "Hell yeah. In the middle of raisin country. A place smaller than this. Definitely not as scenic either. "

"I still don't understand why you're here."

"Don't you?" He stood and pulled her out of the chair, yanking her into his arms. Her body fired up like a raging storm at his touch.

She refused to hope, refused to give flight to her rampant thoughts of why he might be here. "No. I don't."

"Gonna make me spell it out for you?"

She swept her hand over the unruly lock of hair which had fallen across his forehead. Frankly, she didn't care why he was here, she was just so damn glad to see him she could have cried. But still, she wanted to know. "Yup."

"Fine then. I missed you. I haven't slept for a month, I can't write, and despite the fact I swore I'd forget you, there's no fucking way it's going to happen."

"Why?" Her heart soared, but she still needed to hear the words.

Instead of telling her, he showed her. His hands slid to her neck and pulled her lips to his. The kiss was achingly sweet and tender, then increased as his tongue found hers and turned her legs to jelly.

Then he told her. "I love you, Professor Serena Graham."

Tears filled her eyes. This time, she knew he meant it. "I love you too, Michael Donovan."

"I can't live without you. So now what do we do?"

She didn't know, and didn't care. Right now she was trying to recover from the fact that he was here and he loved her. "I have no idea."

"I can write anywhere, you know. And I kind of like this small town atmosphere. Think it would scandalize the community if a jaded erotic crime writer moved in with the literature professor?"

Was this all a dream? Not only had she found the man of her dreams, but he was willing to move to be with her. "I could care less what anyone thinks any longer. This is my life, and I'll live it any way I choose. Besides, I can teach anywhere too. We could live in California."

His eyes widened. "Land of sex, sin and debauchery?"

She laughed. "Sounds right up our alley."

He swept her mouth into a passionate kiss and ran his hands over her body. Hands that knew her so well—every inch of her. Heat and moisture pooled between her legs.

"We'll figure out the logistics later. Right now, I need to fuck you so bad I can't breathe."

With a shaky breath she said, "Great minds think alike. I need you Michael. I haven't been able to sleep or function since I left Paradise. Make love to me. Right here, right now."

His eyes widened. "You're joking. Here? Now?"

She graced him with a seductive smile and licked her lips. "Right here. I want you to fuck me on my desk. Hard."

One of the things she loved the most about him was his lack of shock. As if she'd just asked him to hand her a pencil, he nodded. He stepped away and quickly closed the door to her office and locked it, then shut the blinds. His eyes darkened to a stormy blue as he approached her, already unzipping his jeans. "My pleasure, Professor."

Sweeping the pile of papers off her desk, he lifted her easily and laid her on the desk, unbuttoning her blouse with deft, quick fingers.

"Hurry," she cried, needing him so bad she knew she would come in an instant. The ache to feel his cock pulsated within her.

He swept his hands up her skirt and pulled her skimpy panties down her legs, then hiked the skirt up over her hips and penetrated her in a quick thrust.

He was hard and hot and fucking perfect.

"Miss me?" he groaned as he swept her lips in a heated kiss.

"Yes, desperately," she cried as he stroked her hard.

"Touch yourself and think about me?"

She whimpered and moaned and said, "Daily."

When his lips found hers again she threaded her fingers through his hair and pulled roughly. He pounded her relentlessly and she had to bite back the cries that threatened to spill from her throat.

Instantly the contractions squeezed her. The orgasm burst through her and she lifted her hips and wrapped her legs around his waist, holding him tight as he groaned and came hard and fast inside her.

When it was over and they could both breathe again, Michael swept her hair away from her face and kissed her gently, his eyes full of the love she knew was genuine.

"Let's go home," he said.

"Yes. Let's do that."

Serena smiled at him and held him close, knowing the real adventure of her life was about to begin.

Why an electronic book?

We live in the Information Age — an exciting time in the history of human civilization, in which technology rules supreme and continues to progress in leaps and bounds every minute of every day. For a multitude of reasons, more and more avid literary fans are opting to purchase e-books instead of paper books. The question from those not yet initiated into the world of electronic reading is simply: *Why?*

1. *Price.* An electronic title at Ellora's Cave Publishing and Cerridwen Press runs anywhere from 40% to 75% less than the cover price of the exact same title in paperback format. Why? Basic mathematics and cost. It is less expensive to publish an e-book (no paper and printing, no warehousing and shipping) than it is to publish a paperback, so the savings are passed along to the consumer.

2. *Space.* Running out of room in your house for your books? That is one worry you will never have with electronic books. For a low one-time cost, you can purchase a handheld device specifically designed for e-reading. Many e-readers have large, convenient screens for viewing. Better yet, hundreds of titles can be stored within your new library — on a single microchip. There a variety of e-readers from different manufacturers. You can also read e-books on your PC or laptop computer. (Please note that Ellora's Cave does not endorse any specific brands.

You can check our websites at www.ellorascave.com or www.cerridwenpress.com for information we make available to new consumers.)

3. *Mobility.* Because your new e-library consists of only a microchip within a small, easily transportable e-reader, your entire cache of books can be taken with you wherever you go.

4. *Personal Viewing Preferences.* Are the words you are currently reading too small? Too large? Too... ANNOYING? Paperback books cannot be modified according to personal preferences, but e-books can.

5. *Instant Gratification.* Is it the middle of the night and all the bookstores near you are closed? Are you tired of waiting days, sometimes weeks, for bookstores to ship the novels you bought? Ellora's Cave Publishing sells instantaneous downloads twenty-four hours a day, seven days a week, every day of the year. Our webstore is never closed. Our e-book delivery system is 100% automated, meaning your order is filled as soon as you pay for it.

Those are a few of the top reasons why electronic books are replacing paperbacks for many avid readers.

As always, Ellora's Cave and Cerridwen Press welcome your questions and comments. We invite you to email us at Comments@ellorascave.com or write to us directly at Ellora's Cave Publishing Inc., 1056 Home Avenue, Akron, OH 44310-3502.

COMING TO A BOOKSTORE NEAR YOU!

ELLORA'S CAVE

Bestselling Authors Tour

Made in the USA
Lexington, KY
18 January 2010